He **hul** **from a nearby alley to attack Robbie.**

Had she seen someone like that before at one of her shows? Had someone like that been following her? Sending those fear-inducing notes?

Those thoughts kept her from sleep until she focused on the occasional sound of computer keys tapping and movement outside her door.

It was reassuring to know Robbie was out there.

In the last week, during the investigation, they'd spent some time together and it had reinforced her earlier impressions of him as a good guy. The kind a woman could rely on.

Tonight he'd shown her a different side. A tough side that hinted that he might be up for any kind of challenge.

But would he be up for whatever trouble was coming her way?

DEFENDED
BY THE BODYGUARD

CARIDAD PIÑEIRO

Harlequin

INTRIGUE

To my daughter Samantha, I am so proud of all you've accomplished and know you will do many great things.
May little Axel bring you lots of joy and happiness!

 Harlequin®
INTRIGUE™

Recycling programs for this product may not exist in your area.

ISBN-13: 978-1-335-69009-8

Defended by the Bodyguard

Copyright © 2025 by Caridad Piñeiro Scordato

For questions and comments about the quality of this book, please contact us at CustomerService@Harlequin.com.

TM and ® are trademarks of Harlequin Enterprises ULC.

 Harlequin Enterprises ULC
22 Adelaide St. West, 41st Floor
Toronto, Ontario M5H 4E3, Canada
www.Harlequin.com

Printed in Lithuania

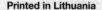 MIX
Paper | Supporting responsible forestry
FSC® C021394

New York Times and USA TODAY bestselling author **Caridad Piñeiro** is a Jersey girl who just wants to write and is the author of nearly fifty novels and novellas. She loves romance novels, superheroes, TV and cooking. For more information on Caridad and her dark, sexy romantic suspense and paranormal romances, please visit www.caridad.com.

Books by Caridad Piñeiro

Harlequin Intrigue

Crooked Pass Security

Cliffside Kidnapping
Defended by the Bodyguard

South Beach Security: K-9 Division

Sabotage Operation
Escape the Everglades
Killer in the Kennel
Danger in Dade

South Beach Security

Lost in Little Havana
Brickell Avenue Ambush
Biscayne Bay Breach

Cold Case Reopened
Trapping a Terrorist
Decoy Training

Visit the Author Profile page at Harlequin.com.

CAST OF CHARACTERS

***Robert (Robbie) Whitaker*—**Robbie is a computer genius who works with his younger sister, Sophie, at South Beach Security. He has a close relationship with Sophie, and together they rely on the latest technologies to help solve crimes and protect vulnerable people.

***Selene Reilly*—**Selene has suffered abuse from her now ex-husband and two mountain men who kidnapped her while on a hike. Selene is rebuilding her life and is having success as a musician in Denver. She sings at a popular bar, and a music producer is interested in signing her to her record label.

***Lily*—**A gray-and-white pit bull mix, Lily was adopted by Robbie and Selene to provide companionship and protection to Selene.

***Ryder Hunt*—**Ryder works for the Colorado Bureau of Investigation. A former marine who served in Afghanistan, Ryder has joined the bureau as an investigator and has been called to investigate when important evidence from a local rape case goes missing from the CBI Forensics Lab and also from the Biometric Identification and Records division, threatening the prosecution of the case.

***Josefina (Sophie) Whitaker*—**Sophie is a computer genius who is working with her cousins at South Beach Security in Miami. An MIT graduate, she and her older brother, Robbie, had started a business together in Silicon Beach developing games and apps and also doing ethical hacking before joining South Beach Security with their Gonzalez cousins.

Chapter One

Stars exploded across his vision as a fist connected with his left eye.

Robbie Whitaker blocked the second blow with his forearm.

As the man struck out again, years of training took over.

Robbie swept aside the punch flying toward his head and delivered a sharp jab to the man's solar plexus.

A pained grunt erupted from his attacker, and he stumbled back just as Selene Reilly shouted out, "I'm calling 9-1-1."

That dissuaded his masked attacker from continuing. Half-bent, still in pain from Robbie's blow, he muttered a curse, whirled around and ran off.

Robbie was about to give chase when Selene laid a hand on his arm, holding him back.

"You're bleeding," she said, face pale. Her bright, almost electric blue eyes were wide with a combination of fear and worry.

The warmth of blood trickling down his face finally registered, as did the pain around his left eye and cheek.

He brushed his fingers along his face, and they came away wet with blood.

Blasting out an expletive, he glanced toward where their attacker had escaped and said, "You should have let me follow him."

Selene shook her head so vehemently that it made the locks

of her dark, nearly seal-black hair dance across her shoulders. "It's too dangerous, especially since we now suspect that someone is after you and your sister Sophie."

He hated to admit that she was right, but since their investigation into his parents' kidnapping had revealed that his sister Sophie and he were the new targets, he had to be more cautious. But there was something about this attack that niggled at his gut. He could have sworn that the curse the man had muttered had been directed at Selene.

Plus, if someone had wanted him dead, it would have been easy to take a shot at him as they walked down the street toward the condo where Selene lived. Or knife him as they came close enough for that punch that had surprised him.

A hands-on attack like this one struck him as far more personal.

He kept that to himself as he said, "You're right. Let's head to your condo."

"*Rhea's* condo. She's just letting me stay there while I decide what to do," Selene said and walked beside him for the short walk to the building that housed Selene's twin sister's condo and art gallery.

"It's nice that you have her support. Family is so important," he said, familiar with the tragedy that had touched Selene's life. His cousin Jackson, then a detective in Regina, had brought his sister Sophie and him into the investigation surrounding Selene's disappearance over a year earlier.

"It is. I don't know how I would have gotten over the kidnapping and…stuff…without Rhea and Jax," Selene said, voice choked with emotion at the memory of what had happened.

"Now we're family too, since Jax married your sister," he said. He held back from asking for more information since it must be upsetting to discuss her abduction and abuse. Instead, he turned the discussion to a happier topic. "I hear your music career is doing well here in Denver."

A ghost of a smile drifted across her lips and her eyes lost some of the pain that had darkened them just seconds before. "It is. I've had lots of gigs at a well-known bar and my songs and album are selling well. I even have a producer who's interested in my work."

He continued the discussion on her singing career as they walked the final block to the condo, but he kept an eye open for any signs of danger. He'd obviously been lax before and he wasn't about to let another attack happen on his watch.

Barely a few minutes later, they were at the front door to the small condo building above Rhea Whitaker's art gallery. "I understand you work part-time in the gallery when you're not singing," he said as Selene used a key card to open the condo's front door.

"It's the least I can do to help my sister after all that she did to reopen the case about my disappearance. And I'm so happy that she found Jackson. They're so good together."

He was grateful as well. He'd never seen his cousin so happy, especially as Jackson and Rhea awaited the birth of their first child in a few weeks.

"He is happy. I'm sure once we solve the case surrounding my parents' kidnapping, everything will be back to normal," he said while they waited for an elevator to take them up to the penthouse floor where Selene was.

Selene glanced at him from the corner of her eye and said, "I guess you'll go back to Miami once the investigation is finished."

It had been on his mind for days. He'd noticed the growing attraction between his sister Sophie and Ryder Hunt, the Colorado Bureau of Investigation agent who was helping solve their parents' kidnapping and the theft of evidence from the Regina Police Department. And truth be told, with every minute that he spent with Selene, he found himself more and more attracted to the beautiful musician.

"Maybe. It'll depend on how my parents are doing," he said, praying that his parents hadn't been harmed during the kidnapping and would soon be free.

With another side-eyed and slightly shy glance, Selene said, "You're more than welcome to stay here as long as you want. Rhea's condo is spacious."

The elevator ding helped him recover from the shock of the invitation. He hoped he wasn't misreading the signals he'd been getting that Selene might also be interested in him.

Once they'd boarded the elevator, he peered down at her, trying to see if he was right about the growing attraction.

A becoming flush colored her cheeks as she looked away and wrung her hands nervously. Wanting to alleviate her discomfort, he said, "Thank you. I might take you up on that offer."

Her lips broadened into a smile, and she nodded. "Great. That would be great."

The elevator doors swished open as they reached the topmost floor. They exited and walked down the hall to Rhea's condo. Selene badged them in, and they had barely entered when his phone blurted out the ringtone for his cousin Jackson, now Regina's Chief of Police.

He answered immediately and put the call on speaker. "Please tell me you have good news."

"I do. I'm with your parents. They escaped and are in good shape. Officers Dillon and Rodriguez are taking them back to Regina while I wait for backup from CBI and the CSI unit to gather evidence."

"Be safe, Jax. Remember you have a baby on the way," Selene said, worried about the dangers that her brother-in-law might be facing from the kidnappers.

"Believe me, I'm not taking any chances," Jackson replied.

"What about Sophie and Ryder?" Robbie asked.

"They're at a casino following up another lead. I hope to hear from them soon," Jackson advised.

"Keep us posted and most of all, stay safe," Robbie said and ended the call.

"That's good news," Selene said, but despite her words, Robbie detected underlying worry.

"What's wrong?" he asked and was about to brush a knuckle beneath her chin to urge her to meet his gaze, but she flinched and stepped back.

"Nothing. It's nothing," she said and then worried her lower lip with her perfect front teeth.

He could see it was something she didn't want to share just yet.

"Whatever it is—" he began but his phone erupted again with another call, this time from his sister Sophie.

"What's up, Soph?" he said, hating that her call had interrupted his discussion with Selene.

"Ryder and I have identified another possible suspect—a casino owner with ties to our two suspects. We think there's money laundering going on and that the money may be going to some PACs for an election campaign."

"Let me guess. You want me to follow the dark money," he said, knowing his sister almost better than he knew himself.

"We do. Listen, I have to go. We'll talk in the morning," she said and abruptly hung up, clearly in a rush.

"What happens now?" Selene said, having overheard Sophie's instructions.

"We put a bow on this investigation by tying up all the loose ends. If this casino dude is behind any dark money flowing to our suspect, we find out how he got that money and what that has to do with kidnapping my parents," he explained as he walked over to a table, laid his knapsack on one of the chairs and dropped his duffle to the floor.

"You think you can do that?" she asked, brows furrowed over those engaging blue eyes.

"I can. It might take some time but if I recall correctly, you offered to let me stay for a little while," he said with a grin.

The furrows disappeared and an inviting smile lightened her features. "I did. But it's late and I have to work in the morning. Let's take care of that cut and get you cleaned up first."

"Lead the way," he said and held his hand out in invitation.

She guided him down the hall to the bathroom and he sat on the toilet seat and waited for her to find first aid supplies from the vanity and medicine cabinet.

Working efficiently, she laid out the various materials but winced as she was about to apply a gauze pad to the cut on his face.

"It might hurt."

"That's okay," he said and tried to control his flinch as she used the antiseptic-soaked gauze on his brow.

She gently washed away the blood on his face and the wound, then applied some antibiotic salve before covering it with a bandage.

"There," she said with a satisfied smile.

He brushed his fingers across the bandage and found the area was slightly tender to the touch. He didn't doubt that he'd have a black eye in the morning, which would require some explaining during their morning video meeting.

"Thank you. I know you want to get some rest—"

"Yes, I do, so let me show you to your room."

With a nod, he rose, hurried back to the living area and grabbed his duffle. "Is it okay to work at the dining table?"

"Of course," she replied and gestured to a small hallway off the open concept living area with her arm. The multiple bracelets at her wrist jangled almost musically with the movement.

As they walked there, she said, "I'm using Rhea's old room.

The guest bedroom is across the hall, and you know where the bathroom is now."

"Great," he said and stood at the guest room door, shifting from foot to foot as she went to her room, barely an arm's length away.

She stood at her door uneasily, wringing her hands again.

He stepped closer and drifted his hand across hers, wanting to ease her discomfort, but her body tensed at his touch. "Whatever is bothering you might be easier to handle if you shared it."

Chapter Two

Selene wished she could share everything weighing on her heart but with so much already happening with the investigation, the last thing Robbie or Jackson needed was another problem. Again.

"It's nothing. And I'm glad you might be staying in Denver a little longer. It'll be nice to have company. Rhea hasn't been around as much now that she's almost due," she said and surprised herself by twining her fingers with his, seeking his touch. It had been too long since she'd experienced a man's gentle touch.

Robbie's almost aqua gaze locked on hers, so intense she had to look away.

He shifted so that his face was in her line of sight and in a soft and patient tone he said, "Whatever it is—"

"It's nothing," she reiterated and hated the deception. She prided herself on being honorable and trustworthy, which made the lie bitter on her tongue.

A heavy sigh gusted from him before he dipped his head and said, "Just remember I'm here for you. We're *all* here for you."

She forced a smile. "I know."

He pointed to the dining table and said, "I'll be there if you need me."

"G'night," she said, then hurried into her room and closed

the door before leaning against it as her mind raced with all that had happened that night. With the secret she had been keeping from everyone to not burden them…again.

Rhea and Jackson had come to her rescue well over a year earlier when they'd freed her from the abductors who had kept her for months to cook, clean and satisfy their physical needs. Before that, Rhea had constantly worried about the mental abuse heaped on Selene by her now ex-husband.

The last thing Selene wanted was to bring them more worries, but she'd be a fool to ignore that trouble was knocking on her doorstep once more.

She pushed off the door, hurried to the nightstand and took out a small jewelry box. She sat on the bed and with a shaky hand, she opened the box where she had tucked the last few notes left by her secret admirer.

She hadn't kept the first notes that had been left for her at the bar where she sang, writing them off as just fan letters. She'd almost been flattered by the attention at first since it had been so long since she'd had any positive male interest.

But then the notes had become a little more obsessive. Fearfully demanding. And the last one had sent a chill through her.

I'm going to get you, bitch.

She thought that she'd heard Robbie's attacker utter something similar during the fight but wasn't sure.

Besides, considering that the current investigation involving the kidnapping of Robbie's parents and the threat they'd uncovered to him and his sister, it seemed more likely the attack was related to that and not to the notes she held in her hands.

Shaky hands, she now realized and sucked in a breath to quell her fears.

The attack had nothing to do with me, she told herself over and over.

But as she tucked the notes back into the jewelry box and slipped it into the nightstand, the little voice in her head chastised her.

You know it's about you, Selene. You know it is, the little voice said.

No, it isn't. It isn't. I won't be a burden to my family again, Selene argued.

The little voice quieted but the damage had been done.

As she washed up and changed into her pajamas, the worrisome thoughts lingered like the bad smell from garbage left too long in the alley behind the bar where she performed.

Lying in bed in the dark, she replayed that night's events and the general shape of the attacker as he slipped from a nearby alley to attack Robbie.

Had she seen someone like that before at one of her shows? Had someone like that been following her? Sending those fear-inducing notes?

Those thoughts kept her from sleep until she focused on the occasional sound of computer keys tapping and movement outside her door.

It was reassuring to know Robbie was out there.

She'd met him more than once when he and his family visited their Whitaker cousins for vacation. He'd struck her as intelligent and friendly. Handsome with his wavy coffee-brown hair, intense blue eyes and dimples that often framed a boyish grin.

In the last week, during the investigation, they'd spent some time together and it had reinforced her earlier impressions of him as a good guy. The kind a woman could rely on.

Tonight, he'd shown her a different side. A tough side that hinted that he might be up for any kind of challenge.

But would he be up for whatever trouble was coming her

way? She wondered that as fatigue finally made her eyes drift closed, and she slipped into a troubled sleep.

FOLLOW THE MONEY, his sister had said, and Robbie was doing just that.

The first step was the Federal Election Commission database. Simple enough to pull up a list of those who had given money to either support or oppose State Senator Oliver, their prime suspect in his parents' kidnapping.

The list wasn't all that long and included several names he was familiar with from larger elections: unions, political parties and assorted PACs. But other names jumped off the page and he wrote those down for further investigation.

Digging around, he discovered various websites providing information on how to follow the money for election campaigns. Reading through them, it shocked him to know just how relatively easy it was to create groups that funneled money to influence elections in ways that most people would never realize.

He didn't need to look too deeply on the various websites to locate links to access the IRS 990 forms filed by the groups to explain their income and expenses.

Surprisingly, the lists of expenses weren't all that detailed and went to generic payouts like advertising and promotion, which could have been used for anything. Including hiring goons to kidnap his parents or hack into computer databases to destroy evidence.

But there was one common thread he realized as he looked over each 990 form. The same treasurer's name and post office box appeared on multiple forms.

Way too much coincidence.

Searching the Colorado Secretary of State for each of the entities, the same name popped up as the registered agent.

No longer just coincidence, he thought. He searched the web for the man behind what were clearly shell companies.

He didn't have to search for long.

The man was a lawyer in Denver who counted among his many clients the casino being investigated by Sophie and Ryder.

Robbie didn't doubt that the money being sent to Oliver through the PACs was part of some kind of money laundering operation. Chances were, Oliver was then paying out that money as a campaign expense of some kind, making dirty money clean.

He reached for his phone and was about to call his sister when he realized what time it was—almost one in the morning. While he was pleased with the information he'd gathered, it could wait until their morning meeting.

He stood and was about to close his laptop when something made him stop.

That niggling sensation from earlier about tonight's attack was back.

It struck him again that the attack had been personal but not directed toward him, although he'd been the recipient of the violence.

That muttered statement, something like "I'll get you," warned that the target had been Selene.

And if his gut was right, to keep Selene safe he would need to know more about all that had happened to her in the last couple of years.

Which meant that no matter how late it was, he had to dig for that info in any way he could.

He sat back down and went to work, accessing files from the Regina Police Department database.

The original entries in the file detailed the discovery of Selene's car by the lake in Regina. All the initial investigations had pointed to the fact that Selene had possibly killed herself, including a message to her twin sister, Rhea, that said something to the effect that she couldn't take it anymore. Because of that, the initial investigation had been closed as a suicide.

But her Rhea had refused to accept that decision, insisting that their unique twin connection indicated her sister was still alive.

Rhea had returned to Regina six months after her sister's disappearance and pushed Robbie's cousin Jackson, then a detective with the police department, to reopen the case. Once Jackson had started to have his doubts as well, he'd called in Sophie and Robbie to assist on the case, offering expertise on LIDAR searches and identifying possible locations where Selene might be found.

Luckily, Rhea had been right. Selene hadn't committed suicide. She'd been kidnapped by two mountain men who had been keeping her hostage on the mountainside. The work that Sophie and he had done had helped find and free Selene.

That much was clear from the detailed report that Jackson had added to the file before it had been closed for the final time.

Too detailed, he thought, his stomach churning as he read about the abuse Selene had suffered at the hands of the two men.

It was almost too intimate to read the facts and yet he felt compelled to do it, needing to know how those events had affected Selene. Whether those events might somehow be the reason for tonight's attack.

He wanted to keep researching but he was furiously battling to stay alert. He didn't want to miss anything important because he was tired.

Rising, he shut his laptop and hurried to his room, hoping to get at least a few hours of rest before this morning's meeting.

As he neared the bedrooms, he hesitated, walked over to her door and skimmed his fingers against the wood, almost as if he were touching her. Offering comfort for all that had happened to her and wishing that Selene's pain and troubles were over.

His gut told him he was wrong. That Selene was in trouble once again.

But whatever it was, he intended to be there for her.

Chapter Three

Selene sat silently as the team ran through all the developments in their current investigation and from what she could see, it was just a matter of putting a bow on it as Robbie had indicated the night before.

But as he mentioned last night's attack and his concerns that it didn't have anything to do with their current investigation, her blood ran cold. She looked away from him as he gazed in her direction, afraid he'd see the truth in her eyes.

He didn't press her, intent on listening to the developments in the investigation and how the FBI and CBI would be taking it over, leaving his cousin Jackson to finish up with only some of the local aspects of the case, and, of course, the imminent birth of his son.

She breathed a sigh of relief that all had gone well with the investigation and hoped that last night's incident was just an aberration.

Not surprisingly, his sister Sophie added her news about returning to Denver with CBI Agent Ryder Hunt and it was clear that the two were truly in love.

A second later, his parents, now free of their kidnappers, advised that they would also be staying in Regina before possibly retiring from the NSA.

She was happy for Robbie's sister and glad that his parents were safe and taking some time off after their recent ordeal.

It came as no surprise when Robbie immediately piped up to also say that he'd be staying on in Denver and glanced in her direction, a decidedly loving expression on his face.

How she wished she could believe in happily-ever-after, but she'd suffered too much in her life to hope for that in her future. And when Robbie repeated his worry that last night's attack wasn't related to the investigation they'd just closed, fear chilled her gut again.

She whipped her gaze away from Robbie's intense look and sat quietly as the team ended the call with promises that Sophie and his parents would soon be visiting them in Denver.

Robbie closed his laptop, swiveled slightly in his chair and continued to peer at her as he said, "I know you don't want to admit that attack has to do with you."

"I don't," she agreed, then finally met his gaze. "I don't want anyone to worry about me again. I've caused everyone too much trouble already."

ROBBIE LAID HIS hand on hers as it rested on the tabletop and hated that she recoiled slightly as he did so. But then again, Selene had suffered a great deal of abuse in her short life and that trauma likely lingered. He would have to be careful when dealing with her.

Slowly shifting his hand away, so as not to spook her, he said, "*You* weren't the one causing the trouble, Selene. And the last thing your loved ones would want is to ignore any possible threats to your safety."

She worried her lower lip with her teeth and finally dipped her head hesitantly. "I know, only… I need to get ready for work," she said and bolted from the room.

The slam of her bedroom door warned him not to follow.

Robbie sat there, drumming his fingers on the table as he considered what to do.

He did not doubt that something was up with Selene, which

only reinforced his belief that last night's attack had to do with her and not the investigation they had just closed.

But as he'd thought before, he'd need to be careful—and caring—around Selene because of her past abuse.

And if there was one person who could help him know how to do that, it was his cousin Ricky, a psychologist who worked with the victims of domestic abuse and often helped South Beach Security with cases involving such victims or when they needed a suspect profile.

Needing more privacy for the discussion, mainly because he didn't think Selene would appreciate being the subject of Ricky's psychoanalysis, he headed to the guest room and shut the door.

His cousin, well aware that they were working on an investigation and might need his help, immediately picked up.

"How are your parents? How is the investigation going?" Ricky Gonzalez asked.

"Mami and Papi are fine, luckily, and we've pretty much wrapped up the case," Robbie said.

"Good to hear. We were all so worried about your parents," Ricky said but then quickly added, "So what do you need from me?"

"Do you remember Selene Reilly?" he said, hoping Ricky would recall some of the details of Selene's cold case.

"Rhea's twin sister, right? The one who went missing?" Ricky asked just to confirm.

It was way more than being missing, Robbie thought. He provided Ricky with some of the details of the abuse Selene had suffered at the hands of both her ex-husband and the two mountain men who had abducted her.

"Wow, that's a lot to unpack," Ricky said, followed by a low whistle.

"Yes, wow. I don't know how she's handling all that," Robbie said.

"Probably not well even if she's presenting a good face to the public," Ricky said and then continued. "I work with women who've been abused, both physically and mentally, and as you know, my fiancée Mariela had been mentally abused by her husband."

"I know and I'm guessing it wasn't easy to earn her trust," Robbie said, imagining how hard it might be for someone who'd known such cruelty.

"It wasn't. Women who've been abused can suffer from PTSD and depression. They may exhibit fear in situations where you and I don't see a threat." Ricky paused and sucked in a deep breath, clearly thoughtful. A second later he said, "Why are you asking, Robbie?"

Now it was Robbie's time to delay as he turned that question over in his mind again and again. Finally, he blurted out, "I think I care about her."

Another long pause followed before Ricky said, "Then you have to be especially aware of her physical space and not violate it. You also need to look past the face she's presenting to the outside world because she might not be feeling that inside."

"She seems to be doing well considering all that's happened," Robbie confirmed from what he'd seen of Selene in the past week or so. Even during the attack the night before, she hadn't let fear paralyze her from warning about a 911 call to dissuade their attacker.

"She could be, but she could also be burying all those emotions until one day they all erupt," Ricky said and mimicked the sound of an explosion in emphasis.

In the background, someone called out to his cousin, and Robbie realized that Ricky might be getting ready to go to work.

"I should let you go."

"Thanks. I have a meeting at the women's shelter South Beach Security is sponsoring," Ricky admitted.

Since taking over the helm of South Beach Security, his cousin Trey Gonzalez had moved to expand the agency's reach in many ways. First had been the new K-9 division that had helped so many people over the last few months, and now, a shelter for abused women with the help of his cousin Mia's tech-billionaire husband.

All good things, which made him proud of what his family was able to do to help others.

Much like what the Whitaker side in Colorado was doing since his cousin Jackson had become the Regina Police Chief. He was modernizing the department and adding K-9s who might assist with their work. He hoped that whatever was happening with the state senator, who had been a big supporter of the K-9 unit, wouldn't impact his cousin's plans.

Which made him wonder if getting Selene a dog would help protect her once he went back to Miami. It might even help her deal with any possible issues she might still have. Dogs were often used for therapy since they provided emotional support and companionship.

As he heard a door opening in the hallway, he rushed out and nearly bumped into Selene when she hurried out of her room.

She jumped back in alarm, a hand splayed against her heart. "You scared me."

He held his hands up in apology and took a step back, mindful of Ricky's earlier words about respecting her space. "I'm sorry. I just wanted to catch you before you left."

She mimicked his actions, waving off his apology. "No, I'm sorry. It's just that you surprised me. I'm not good with surprises."

Nodding, he said, "I'll keep that in mind. I don't want to upset you by being here."

She bit her lower lip again in a gesture that was becoming

familiar and warned that she was uncomfortable. But with a shake of her head, she said, "No, it's nice to have company."

He went to skim a hand across her arm to reassure her but, mindful of the discussion he'd just had with his cousin, he held back his instinct to comfort her. He was a toucher by nature and had done that with her earlier. Carelessly, he realized. He wouldn't make that mistake again.

"Do you want me to walk you down to the store?" he asked and shoved his hands in his jeans pockets to keep them to himself.

She gestured with one elegant hand, bracelets jangling on her wrists. She'd added a few rings as well that graced her long artist's fingers.

"It's just downstairs."

With a shrug, he said, "That's fine with me. I wanted to check out the neighborhood."

And make sure that whoever had attacked them the night before wasn't lurking around.

She dipped her head, smiled and said, "Okay. I'd like that."

"Just let me get my knapsack."

While he packed up his laptop, Selene also gathered her things, and it wasn't long before they'd ridden the elevator down and reached the front door.

Her steps slowed as she neared the door and he eased past her and said, "Let me."

He perused the street to make sure it was clear before he stepped out and held the glass door open for her.

She exited the building cautiously, he noted, likewise looking around. It confirmed to him that despite her protestations that nothing was wrong, there was definitely something going on. But he wouldn't press. She'd hopefully share when she was ready.

The walk to Rhea's gallery was short. Just a dozen or

so steps and Robbie lingered as she unlocked the door and stepped inside.

"Mind if I come in? I'd love to see some of Rhea's work," he said and at her nod, he followed her in.

With a wave of her hand in the direction of one wall, she said, "Rhea's art is over there. We also feature other artists that Rhea thinks have potential."

He walked over and stood before the collection of land-scapes, hands on his hips as he considered the artwork. He wasn't an art connoisseur, but you didn't need to be to appreciate the lovely scenes of mountains, lakes or small-town streets done in bold colors and with an impressionistic touch.

"They're beautiful," he said and did a slow swivel to examine the other walls and shelves that held an assortment of artwork, jewelry and sculptures. The styles of the other items were eclectic but selected with a keen eye for design.

And there was something a bit calming about the place, whether it was the soft music Selene had turned on or the fresh scent wafting through the air. He breathed it in, a stress-relieving mix of mint and eucalyptus. Possibly some pine as well.

"I like this place," he said with another leisurely whirl to take in the space.

"I do too," Selene said with a bright smile, obviously comfortable in this environment.

As someone walked in, a customer from the looks of the young woman, he waved at Selene and said, "I'll see you later."

"Later," she called out and did a little wiggle of her ringed fingers in a good-bye wave.

Back out on the street, Robbie did another perusal of the environs to see if there was anything to worry about. Satisfied that Selene would be okay, he walked down the street, a tree-lined pedestrian mall, taking in all the shops, hotels and restaurants along what was one of Denver's top tourist destinations.

Rhea had made a good choice when buying the mixed-use building for her store and the condos above it. The location almost guaranteed steady foot traffic to her art gallery as well as renters who wanted to be close to amenities.

Last night, between the rush from the police station back to the condo and the attack, he hadn't had a chance to appreciate the area. Now he was able to do that, taking in the variety of shops and restaurants along the street. Some were schlocky souvenir shops and chain eateries, but others were more up-scale, like Rhea's gallery. Here and there were pieces of artwork tucked into small alleys. Along walls and storefronts, murals had been placed here and there to tease the eye.

While he appreciated the artwork, in the back of his mind he was also considering how their attacker had hidden in one of the alleys close to the gallery. Also worrisome was an alley near the large bar where Selene sang on the busier weekend nights. He also detoured down a nearby side street and hurried to the building that held a studio where Selene mentioned that she recorded her music.

The tall brick building for the studio housed several different businesses and boasted a colorful mural depicting several different kinds of arts as a homage to the businesses within. Large colorful musical notes twined around paintbrushes, palettes, chisels and sculptures for the other tenants of the building.

He entered and found an unguarded lobby, which didn't please him. It was too easy to get an elevator up to the floor for the recording studio but luckily the door to that space was locked and the hallway had a CCTV setup that he hoped would record anyone coming and going in the space.

Satisfied, he hurried back out and toward the 16th Street Mall once again, alert to his surroundings and any possible dangers.

As he stopped at one coffee shop, he thought he detected

someone following him, though he might just be paranoid. With his knapsack slung over his shoulder and a tray holding his coffee and a trio of donuts to satisfy his sweet tooth, he took a seat with his back to a wall and faced the street, intent on people-watching. Especially for anyone matching his vague recollection of the man who had punched him the night before.

Luckily, no one fit the bill but that didn't alleviate his worries about the attack.

He was sure it had been directed at Selene but only time would tell. For the moment, he'd stay vigilant and do a little more research into Selene's cold case. His gut was telling him that there might be a connection between that and whatever was happening now.

But as he hauled out his laptop as he ate and read through the details again, his heart ached at what Selene had suffered and his appetite disappeared. He promised himself that no matter what it took, he'd make sure she would never have such pain in her life again.

Armed with that conviction, he packed up, tossed his uneaten donuts and hurried back to the store.

Chapter Four

Selene glanced at the wall clock for what had to be the hundredth time in the last hour.

She told herself it wasn't because she'd been hoping that Robbie would return. Or that she'd get a last-minute customer to help pay some of the gallery's expenses.

Although Rhea owned the building where the gallery was housed and earned income from renting the apartments above it, there were still taxes and other things to be paid.

The ring of the bell above the front door snared her attention and a young couple strolled in arm in arm. They were smiling and laughing as they walked to the wall displaying Rhea's artwork. Their gazes skipped across the various canvases on the wall and a second later, they bent their heads together and chatted in hushed tones.

Selene was always conflicted about whether to approach at such a moment. She didn't want to seem pushy, but she also didn't want to ignore them. A salesperson's conundrum.

With a step away from the register, she slowly walked toward them and in a soft voice said, "If I can help you in any way—"

She didn't get to finish as the woman gushed, "We love these landscapes, and we have a new place where that one would be perfect." She pointed to Rhea's painting depicting Regina's downtown area with its quaint shops and homes.

"That's one of my favorites. It's Main Street—"

"In Regina. It's where we met while we were on a ski trip," the man said and gazed at his companion lovingly.

"Such a nice memory for you. Did you want to take it with you, or did you want to have it shipped?" she asked and was thankful the framed canvas was one of the lower ones she could easily reach.

"We'd love to take it," the couple said.

"Wonderful. I'll ring it up and then wrap it up for you but that may take a few minutes."

The woman jerked a thumb out the door. "We can grab a coffee while you pack it up."

"Great," Selene said. She walked the couple to the register and rang up the purchase, pleased that the sale would have a nice impact on the gallery's bottom line.

As the couple strolled out, Robbie hurried in, looking a little windblown and chilled. His cheeks had the ruddy color from the spring chill outside and he held two coffee cups in his hands.

"I thought you might need a late afternoon pick-me-up," he said and handed her one of the coffees.

"Caramel macchiato. No foam. Did I get that right?" he said with a smile that made her stomach do a little flip and brought warmth that had nothing to do with the heat of the coffee.

"Yes, that's so sweet that you remembered," she said and took a welcome sip. The sugar and caffeine would provide much-needed energy since once she passed off the gallery to the night salesperson, she had a studio session to record another song for a new album and demo tape for the producer who was interested in signing her.

He grinned again and dragged a hand through the waves of his tousled hair. "Glad I got it right." Dipping his head toward the door, he said, "A sale, I hope."

She nodded and laid her cup on the counter. "A sale. I have to wrap it up."

"Can I help?" he asked.

"That would be great," she said, and they walked over to the wall where she pointed out the painting the couple had purchased.

Robbie removed it from the wall and back at the register, Selene hurried into the back room for packing supplies.

She laid a large box on the counter, mindful not to knock over their coffee cups. Then she spread out a large piece of kraft paper and some cardboard corners to both protect them and also keep the painting from shifting in the box.

Robbie laid the painting on the kraft paper, stepped back and grabbed his coffee to sip as she worked on wrapping the couple's sale.

"Your sister does lovely work," he said, admiring the painting the couple had chosen.

"She does. She's quite talented," Selene said as she slipped on the protective corners and then wrapped the kraft paper around the painting.

"Talent runs in the family," he said and eyed her, his aqua-colored gaze bright as it settled on her.

Heat rushed to her face, and she downplayed her skill. "How would you know?"

He pointed a finger upward and she realized one of her slower songs was playing in the background. Rhea had insisted that Selene add some of her music to the gallery's playlist and CDs of her album were available for sale as well.

"That and this," he said and showed her the face of his smartphone where his music app displayed her album.

"Thank you," she said and ducked her head down modestly.

SELENE'S EARLIER BLUSH deepened as she shyly looked away. Mindful that it might be too much if he pressed the issue, he said, "Are you almost done with your shift?"

She nodded, taped the last bit of kraft paper and then turned her attention to sealing the box around the canvas.

"I am but I have to head to the recording studio. I've reserved a spot at six."

With a quick look at his watch, he realized she barely had half an hour to get to the studio. Luckily, he knew it wasn't that far to go.

"Would you mind if I walk you there and stay to see how the magic happens? Maybe take you to dinner after?" he said, mindful of letting Selene control what she wanted since in the past that control had been taken from her.

A shy smile drifted across her lips, and she nodded. "I'd like that."

That innocent smile made his heart stutter and if it had been anyone else, he might have leaned in and sampled that smile, but he had to go slow. He had to respect her space and wait for when she was ready. If she was ever ready.

The musical peal of the bell by the front door drew their attention to where customers were walking in, followed by another woman.

"That's my relief and the couple that bought the painting," Selene explained.

"Great. I guess we can go soon," he said and drifted back to let Selene hand over the package and fill in her replacement on the return of another customer for a possible sale.

Once she was done, she went into the back storeroom and returned with her guitar case and purse. Smiling, blue eyes blazing happily, she approached him.

"I'm ready."

"Let me carry that for you," he said and reached for the handle of the guitar case. As he did so, their hands brushed, and she recoiled for a moment before handing him the case and then smoothing her hand over his in an almost apologetic stroke.

"Thank you," she said, a slight sadness dimming the earlier joy in her gaze.

Leaning in slightly, he whispered, "You can trust me, Selene. I won't ever hurt you."

She bit her lower lip and did an abrupt dip of her head before raising an index finger to her head. "I know it in here," she said and then lowered her finger to a spot above her heart. "It's here where it's harder to believe."

He wanted to say that he got it, only how could he?

"When you're ready, I'm here," he said and motioned her in the direction of the front door.

The barest hesitation was followed by a stuttering step in the direction of the door. She took a second, more decisive step and he fell in behind her, following her out the door and on to the pedestrian mall on 16th Street.

They walked side by side, silent for a few minutes, until she said, "I like having you here. It gets lonely sometimes with Rhea gone."

He suspected that after the trauma she'd endured, company helped keep those memories at bay. But he wondered if it wasn't also about that twin thing.

"Is it true that you and Rhea can feel things others can't?"

"Because we're twins?" she said with a side-eyed glance in his direction.

He nodded. "Sophie and I aren't twins, but sometimes it's like we're one person because we're so close."

She dipped her head. "I could see that with you two. Yes, there is a connection between Rhea and me. The whole time that I was…in trouble, I knew Rhea would find me."

Her hesitation, and the way her voice choked up, spoke volumes and he couldn't stop himself from offering a reassuring stroke down her back. To his surprise, she didn't move away, and a half smile crept onto her face.

"What you share is special. You're lucky to have it," he said and as someone brushed by, they knocked the guitar case, making it bang against his leg.

It almost seemed intentional, making him whirl to see who had done it, but caught only a quick glimpse of the man as he slipped into the coffee shop. White, possibly Hispanic, with dark brown hair, a scruffy ZZ-Top-style beard and a black hoodie.

"Something wrong?" Selene asked and tracked his gaze to look back.

He forced a smile, not wanting to worry her, and said, "Nothing. Just thought I saw someone I knew."

And while the man's overall shape and black hoodie were similar to that of last night's attacker, it fit the profile of way too many men.

His explanation seemed to placate her, and they continued their short walk down 16th Street and passed the bar where she played. Music spilled from its doors as some customers strolled into the building.

He waved a hand in the direction of the bar. "How do you like performing there?"

That bright grin returned along with a glimmer in her gaze. "I love it. There's always good energy in the crowd and the owner has been fantastic."

It pleased him to see her joy. He wished she'd always feel that way about her music.

Just a block away from the bar, they turned in the direction of the building for the recording studio. There was little foot traffic along the street and once inside, it was likewise empty.

Robbie worried once again about the lack of security in that portion of the building and in the elevator. The alarm button would do little to stop anyone who intended serious harm.

On the floor for the recording studio, Selene rang a bell to be buzzed into the space.

Inside there was a large stage to one side, a smaller booth

in the center with a microphone dangling down and, along the remaining wall, glass around the recording equipment. Two men were busy making adjustments.

One of the men came bounding out, a broad smile on his face. He was of average height and build with red hair and a scruffy reddish-blond beard that made him look almost elfish. But his clothes screamed grunge with his faded jeans, T-shirt and flannel shirt.

"Great to see you, Selene." The man turned a slightly inquiring look in his direction.

Selene said, "This is my friend, Robbie Whitaker. Robbie, meet Jason Andrews, my recording genius."

Robbie shook the man's hand and said, "Nice to meet you. Is it okay if I stay to see how it's done?"

A reluctant shrug was followed by "Sure."

You didn't need to be a genius to see the man was interested in Selene for more than her music.

Jason gestured to the equipment booth. "Just take a spot in there and stay back while we work."

"Got it," Robbie said with a little salute, but despite that, he followed Selene to the booth with the guitar case. Once she was settled, he said, "Break a leg. That's good luck, right?"

"For actors, I think, but I'll take it," she said with a grin and settled on the stool in the booth, the guitar tucked onto her knee.

He hurried from the room and to the equipment booth where, as instructed, he took a spot off to one side where he would watch Selene as she sang.

He was very grateful that he did as an almost magical transformation slipped over her.

SELENE SLIPPED ON the headphones that would help isolate background noises but also let her focus on her voice in real time so she could make any necessary adjustments to her pitch or volume.

She strummed her hands across the strings and the notes reverberated in her head but more importantly, they reached inside her, awakening parts of her that had been dead for too long.

Whatever pain had existed in her past disappeared with the feel of her fingers against the steel of the strings. Against her heart, the wood of the guitar seemed alive, awakening it, and from within the song came, filled with life and joy but also with that pain.

It was that mix of emotions that made the song so special. So true. And even though this was just the start of the familiar testing of sound levels, she couldn't stop singing just yet.

Especially as her gaze connected with Robbie's across the width of the room.

It wasn't a love song and yet…it was hard not to imagine it being one for him. Unexpected and maybe even unwanted considering the current state of her life. Considering what she was keeping from him.

The voice breaking in over the speakers shattered the moment. "That's beautiful, Selene. Really beautiful," Jason said although she detected a note of annoyance in his tone.

She glided her fingers along the string and frets one last time before pausing. "Thank you, Jason. That means a lot."

Jason nodded with a crooked smile. "We just need to make a few adjustments. We want to send the very best to that Miami producer."

She wanted to send the best as well. The producer who was interested in her work could open a lot of doors for her and while it was a reach that she might sign her on for his record company, she could dream, couldn't she?

"Whatever you need, Jase," she said and returned her attention to Robbie, who grinned and shot her a thumbs-up.

That grin did all kinds of wicked things to her stomach and his approval meant a lot too, which worried her.

After her ex-husband's abuse and that of the mountain men who'd kidnapped her, she'd sworn never to worry about what any man thought of her. It was almost like wanting that approval gave a man control over her.

It was something she'd talked over with the therapist she'd visited for months after her ordeal.

She fought back that feeling, trying to convince herself that Robbie was different. That his approval was different.

"Ready when you are," Jason said and with those words, she let go of her fear and pain and let joy return.

Her eyes fixed on Robbie, she literally sang her heart out, letting all those emotions color the words with a kaleidoscope of emotions.

As she finished there was quiet. Too much quiet for way too long, worrying her that her rendition hadn't worked, but then Jason came across the speakers.

"That was just amazing. Perfect. I'm not sure we need another take of that one."

She blew out the breath she'd been holding. "Whew, you all had me worried."

"No, it was just like Jase said," the other sound tech chimed in.

"If you're ready with the next one, I'll feed in the background music and vocals," Jason said.

She nodded, set aside the guitar and seconds later, the recording they'd worked on over the last few weeks erupted across the headphones. They'd modulated her vocals to create a three-part harmony on the choruses and added digital instruments.

Synchronizing her performance to the recorded track, she let herself go and savor the piece. She swayed and rocked to the romantic beat of it.

Unlike the earlier performance, this one needed some work here and there as Jason asked her to change her tone in spots and up her volume in a key chorus.

But after a few runs, the second recording was in the can.

She packed up her guitar, slipped on her jacket, and met Jason and Robbie who had left the recording booth. "That was great," Jason said and hugged her, but then immediately pulled away, hands held up in apology. "Sorry. I didn't mean anything by that."

"I know, Jason. It's okay," she said, mindful that his reaction hadn't meant to harm or sexualize her.

"Thanks," he said and then clapped his hands together. "I almost forgot. This came for you this morning," he said. He reached into the pocket of his flannel shirt and handed her a small envelope.

Fear chilled her gut as she laid her guitar case on the floor and reached for the envelope, hand shaking as she did so.

The envelope wasn't sealed but her fingers still fumbled as she opened it and took out the note.

Her heart stopped as she read the words.

Next time, bitch.

Chapter Five

Selene staggered, knees going weak, and her face lost all traces of color.

"Selene?" Robbie said and reached for her as she dropped the envelope and note.

As quickly as she'd weakened, a wave of strength seemed to wash over her. She stood upright and said, "I'm okay. Fine, just fine."

Jason had retrieved the note and envelope from the ground. His eyes widened as he read the note and held it out to her in question. "What is this, Selene?"

Selene snatched the papers from him. "Nothing. It's nothing."

"Why don't you let me be the judge of that?" Robbie said and held his hand out for the note.

"It's really nothing. I shouldn't have let it upset me," she said, clutching the papers to her chest.

"Selene, please. You can't mess around with things like this," Jason said, hands held out in pleading, and quickly added, "If not for yourself, think of how others might be hurt."

A guilty look slipped across her features as she turned her gaze on him. "I'm sorry. I never wanted to bring trouble to anyone again."

"What matters most is your being safe," Robbie said and held his hand out once more for the papers.

She worried her lower lip again and with a hesitant nod, handed him the note with a shaky hand.

Robbie accepted it and controlled his reaction to the words on the paper. Very few words but that didn't make them any less threatening.

"Again? Have you gotten more of these?" he asked and raised the note in the air.

Another slow, reluctant dip of her head confirmed his worst fears. "Yes. At first, the notes were flattering, like fan letters. It had been so long since I'd heard anything positive that they were welcome."

"And then?" Robbie prompted.

"Then the tone changed. Got harsher—almost possessive— before the threats started," Selene admitted.

Robbie skewered Jason with his gaze. "Were you aware of this?"

Jason vehemently shook his head. "I wasn't. This note was just shoved under the door. I'd never seen anything like that before."

"Is that right?" Robbie asked and at Selene's nod, he pushed on. "Where did you get the other notes?"

"At the bar. They were left in the backstage area where I prep before performing," Selene admitted. She had wrapped her arms around herself, almost as if by doing so she could hold in all the emotions she must be feeling.

He hated having to press, but he needed to know as much as he could to protect her. "Do you have any ideas who might have left them there?"

She shook her head, sending the strands of her dark hair brushing across her delicate shoulders. "No. I asked around, but no one seemed to know."

Turning his attention to Jason, he said, "I noticed a CCTV camera in the lobby. Any chance I can get the video from it?"

An embarrassed flush suffused Jason's pale skin. "It's a

fake camera. We only put it up to discourage people from breaking in or sleeping in the hallway."

"So if they broke in—" Robbie began but Jason quickly cut him off by pointing to a siren in one corner of the room.

"The alarm would go off and dial our security company. We just couldn't afford the camera and monitoring."

"Got it. I didn't mean to imply you'd done anything wrong. I just need to know how much protection we have for Selene," Robbie said, hands raised to reassure Jason he wasn't trying to judge.

"If you think we should add a camera—"

"I'd recommend it, but for right now, Selene and I should go get some dinner and then decide what to do," he said and lovingly glanced at her, wanting to calm her. He hoped that by doing so he'd get the information he needed to protect her and find the stalker who was threatening her.

"I'm not really hungry," Selene said, voice weak. Her face was still pale.

"I know but you need to eat, and I *am* hungry," he said and as if to prove it, his stomach rumbled loudly.

With a series of abrupt nods, she relented and grabbed her guitar case while he slipped the note and envelope into his jacket pocket. While they might be evidence, he worried that too many people had handled them, and it might be tough to get any fingerprints or other evidence from them.

They walked out of the recording studio and boarded the elevator in silence. When they reached the ground floor, Robbie spread one arm wide to hold Selene back.

He stepped into the lobby to make sure it was safe. Satisfied, he reached for her, and she surprised him by slipping her hand into his.

"You good?" he asked, narrowing his gaze to examine her features.

With a bob of her head and a shrug, she said, "How good

could I be? But I don't want to cause any more trouble for everyone."

It surprised him that she was more worried about what others would be feeling rather than herself.

He took a step closer to her and was relieved when she didn't back away as she had in the past. It was like they'd passed one barrier, but he knew there were many more still in the way because of her past.

"You don't need to worry about us. We can handle whatever it is," he assured her.

SELENE WANTED TO believe him. She truly did. But with Rhea due in a few short weeks, she didn't want to worry her sister.

She laid a hand against his heart, wanting to drive her point home. "Rhea and Jax have both had to deal with a lot because of me. This should be a special time for them, and I don't want to ruin it."

He covered her hand with his and pressed it tighter. So tight she felt the reassuring thump of life beneath her palm, and it brought comfort she hadn't felt in too long, as did his words.

"I promise we'll keep them out of it. Sophie and Agent Hunt should be here any day, and I've got the rest of South Beach Security in Miami that can help."

His stomach rumbled again, lightening the moment since it dragged chuckles from both of them.

"But first, dinner," she said and held up her index finger to reinforce what was the number one item at that moment.

"Dinner. Where would you recommend?" he said and took hold of the hand that had rested on his chest, twining his fingers with hers.

The weight of that, the joining, felt right somehow. For many months after her captivity, she'd shunned any male touch. It had just been too reminiscent of what she'd suffered. Slowly she'd gotten used to it, mostly from men she knew, like Jax and his dad.

Allowing this simple touch from Robbie was…life-affirming and dangerous all at the same time.

But she tamped down her fears to embrace the possibilities for her future.

"There's a nice Italian place not far from here," she said and at his nod, they walked to the front door where he once again made sure the area was clear before they exited.

The walk to the restaurant took them past the messy construction area where the renovations of the pedestrian mall were being completed. It wouldn't be long before the area would completely be back to normal.

Although he wasn't that obvious, she knew Robbie was on alert, not wanting to be surprised as he had been the night before.

At the door, he opened it but peered inside before they stepped through.

The hostess at the podium smiled as she saw Selene but grimaced slightly at Robbie's battered face.

He grinned and joked, "The other guy looks worse. Could we please get a table by the wall?"

The hostess peered at Selene as if asking if that was okay. "Not your usual?" she pressed.

"Not the usual. Thanks, Brooklyn," she confirmed.

The young woman grabbed menus and said, "Follow me."

As requested, Brooklyn took them to a table for two against the far wall of the restaurant, which had an old-school Italian vibe. Dark wood walls made the place feel intimate and the tabletops were covered in sparkling white linens with candles at the center along with small vases with a sprig of flowers. Nothing fancy, which had always made it feel homey to her.

"She didn't sound like she's from Brooklyn," Robbie quipped as he pulled the chair out for her.

"She isn't but her Italian parents, who own the place, are from there. It explains why the food is so authentic," Selene said as she sat.

Robbie joined her but didn't grab the menu, surprising her. "You know what you want?"

"I always get chicken parm at a new Italian place. I figure if they can't get that right, they're not worth another visit," he said with a boyish grin.

Selene laughed and shook her head. "Makes sense. You'll love the chicken parmigiana here."

The waitress came over and they both ordered the chicken parm, rousing some chuckles that confused the server for a moment.

"Just an inside joke, Melissa," Selene told the older woman.

"Anything to drink? We have a nice Chianti today," Melissa said.

ROBBIE NORMALLY APPRECIATED a nice glass of wine with Italian food but with all that was happening, he wanted to stay sharp. But he didn't want to decide for Selene, conscious of those possible control issues his cousin had mentioned.

"Would you like a glass?" he asked.

She shook her head. "Just some pop for me, Melissa."

Robbie glanced at the waitress and echoed the order.

As Melissa was about to walk away, she dipped her head in the direction of another server a few yards away at another table. "Bart's missing you today. You're not in your usual spot."

Robbie tracked Selene's gaze as she peered across the restaurant at the man. In his thirties, he was just six feet with a lean, muscular build. A well-trimmed beard covered a strong jaw and as the man faced them, he smiled.

Handsome, which annoyed Robbie. Maybe because as the man set his sights on Selene, his interest was obvious.

Bart closed his order pad and sauntered over with a bit of swagger and daggers in his gaze when it met Robbie's for a split second before locking on Selene.

"It's good to see you, Selene. How are you doing?" Bart said. His arms were crossed against his chest, making his muscles appear even larger. He was clearly trying to make an impression on Selene and Robbie's annoyance flared into full jealousy.

"I'm doing well. How about you?" she asked, her tone friendly.

"Better than your friend," Bart quipped and flicked a dismissive hand in Robbie's direction.

Robbie reined in anger and since his gut was telling him something was off with the man, he said, "Black eyes were worth it to protect Selene. Would you do the same or are all those muscles just for show?"

Bart peered at Selene, his dark eyes wide in surprise—but Robbie wondered if it was a fake response.

"Is that true? Someone attacked you?" Bart asked.

Selene's earlier joy faded and with a curt dip of her head, she brusquely said, "Yes."

Bart raked a hand through the short strands of his dark hair, agitated. "I wish I'd been there."

"No need, I was," Robbie said just as Melissa approached the other man.

"Bart, your order's ready," she said and offered an apologetic look at Selene and him, aware that the other server might be interrupting what was supposed to be a dinner for two.

"I'll have your order shortly," she said and with another glare at Bart, they both hurried off.

"Was that a testosterone contest?" Selene said with a chuckle that lightened the earlier mood.

Robbie pursed his lips. "You might say that. He rubs me the wrong way."

Selene scrutinized Bart as he carried plates over to a couple at another table. "Is he too big? Too muscular?"

The attack had happened so quickly that he hadn't registered much about his assailant, but Selene had gotten a clearer view. "You'd know better than I would. I only got a glimpse of his fist," he kidded, wanting to keep the lighter mood.

Selene wagged her head from side to side. "I'm not sure. To be honest, it was a blur."

As it had been for him, which was why he'd been hoping for some CCTV footage, but during his walk he'd realized there probably weren't many nearby cameras that could help.

"I know Rhea has cameras in the store to protect against shoplifters, but I'd like to put in some other cameras to face the street and door to the condos."

"I'm sure she'd be fine with that, but I'll call to confirm once we're home."

Home. With her. It sounded more appealing than he would have thought less than a week ago. She'd made that kind of impression on him and as his gaze met hers across the intimate space of the table, he detected—or at least he hoped he did—a similar feeling in her.

That was confirmed as she reached across the table and laid her hand on his.

The moment disappeared like windblown smoke when the waitress returned with large plates of cheese-covered breaded chicken cutlets piled on high beds of spaghetti and drowned in red sauce.

"Looks as wonderful as always," Selene said.

"Smells great," Robbie said and clapped his hands in appreciation, hunger driving away his earlier want.

He dug into the food with a satisfied murmur, dragging a chuckle from Selene as she approached her food slightly more delicately.

"I guess it's true," she said and slipped a small piece of chicken into her mouth.

"What's true?" he asked after swallowing his mouthful of pasta.

"That the way to a man's heart is through his stomach," she said with a siren's smile.

"Only if it's you who's serving it to me," he said and gazed at her intensely, wanting no misunderstandings about his feelings.

The blush on her face acknowledged she understood but they quickly turned their attention to the food.

He was grateful to see that the threatening note that had been left for her hadn't affected her appetite or demeanor for the most part. It spoke to her resilience, but he shouldn't have been surprised.

She'd survived so much already—more than most men or women could have endured—and here she was, rebuilding her life and reaching for her dreams.

He just hoped he'd be able to help keep her safe while she did so.

Which had him looking in Bart's direction again and wondering if the server's infatuation with Selene was something Robbie should worry about.

Chapter Six

Despite Selene's earlier upset over her stalker's note, the delightful dinner with Robbie had been almost magical, Bart notwithstanding.

In the past, she hadn't read too much into Bart's attention since her choice of making her usual spot in his serving area had been one of chance. She'd merely liked being able to people-watch out the window in that part of the restaurant and over the last year or so, they'd gotten friendly. Restaurant-friendly, if you could call it that.

Although come to think of it, she'd seen him at one of her performances, which was unusual since most restaurant servers liked to work on Fridays and weekends when it was busier and they could boost their salaries with tips.

She quickly looked in Bart's direction as Robbie and she left, contemplating whether he was at all similar to the man who had thrown the punches at Robbie and threatened her.

She could no longer deny that the man had said, "I'll get you, bitch."

Just like in the last few notes that had been left for her.

At the door, Robbie opened it and searched the street before holding his hand out to lead her outside.

The weight of his hand in hers was comforting, bringing surprise again at how his touch didn't bring alarm or upset.

Definitely good progress on her journey to a new life.

There wasn't any hint of tension in his hand or body as they walked but it was impossible not to notice that he was on high alert, scanning the area all around them as they strolled back to the condo. At the building's glass doors, he peered inside and then shifted to protect her back when she used her key card to open the door.

They entered and rushed to the elevator, which came down quickly since it was too late for her elderly neighbors and too early for the hipsters in the building to be going out.

Robbie shielded her as the elevator doors opened and, comfortable that it was clear, he gently tugged on her hand to urge her in beside him.

Barely minutes later, he repeated the gesture as she opened the door to Rhea's condo.

"Safe and sound," he said with a relieved sigh once he'd done a complete reconnoiter of all the rooms in the condo.

But as relieved as he sounded, his ocean-colored gaze was dark and turbulent as he fixed it on her and took her hand once again. "I know you probably don't want to talk about this—"

"I don't but I understand it's something we have to do," she admitted reluctantly.

Robbie nodded and forced a smile to reassure her. "You said you had gotten other notes. Can I see them?"

Gritting her teeth, she fought back tears as she nodded. "I'll get them."

She rushed off to her room and snagged the jewelry box from where she kept it hidden in the nightstand. When she returned to the dining room table, she noticed that Robbie was putting a kettle on the stove.

At her questioning look, he said, "I always find tea at night calms me. What about you?"

"A cup would be nice," she said, then laid the jewelry box on the table and joined him in the kitchen, taking out mugs, tea bags and honey from the cabinets so they could fix their beverages.

"Milk or cream?" she asked as she stood at the fridge.

"Cream, please," he said, and she pulled out the half-and-half and laid it on the counter beside their mugs.

They stood there, arms brushing, in companionable silence until the shrill whistle of the tea kettle said it was time.

With water poured, tea bags swimming, honey sweetening and cream topping it all off, they hurried to the dining room table to work.

Selene's gut did a little twist as Robbie set down his mug and reached for the jewelry box.

"May I?" he said and met her gaze, searching for any sign of reluctance.

She bit her lower lip and shakily nodded, unable to speak past the turmoil in her gut.

SELENE'S BODY ALMOST vibrated with tension as Robbie reached for the small jewelry box.

It reminded him of one that Sophie once had but hers had a little ballerina that would twirl around while tinny music spilled out.

There was no happy little ballerina. No music as he opened it and saw the pile of about a dozen or so envelopes.

They were similar to the note he had slipped into his jacket pocket earlier.

He picked up his knapsack and placed it on a seat beside him. Opening it, he extracted his laptop and laid it on the table and then jerked some white cotton gloves from a pack he kept there for evidence protection and collection. He also kept a pack of nitrile gloves, but they were so thin that they might still impart his fingerprints to the notes.

He slipped on the gloves even while thinking that the paper had been handled by so many people it wouldn't really help.

But he didn't want to risk losing any DNA or fingerprints on the paper that might help identify Selene's stalker and his attacker.

The ivory-colored envelopes were note-sized and very high quality. The note cards were thick, likely made of cotton, and had a border in navy blue. The liner of the envelope had a matching pinstripe, and the stalker hadn't sealed the notes to avoid any DNA transfer from his saliva.

The design struck him as classic and masculine.

Taking a guess, he opened his laptop, visited the website of a well-established stationery company and searched through their offerings.

Bingo, he thought as he found the identical design on the website. *Good and bad*, he thought, and turned his laptop so Selene, who had been sitting at his side and anxiously sipping her tea, could see the screen.

"Are you familiar with this company?" he asked.

"Crane?" she asked and nodded. "We carry some of their products in the gallery but so do some of the other high-end shops in town."

"And they could have ordered it from the website but at least we have something to go on, especially if we can get some fingerprints off the notes," Robbie explained and examined the handwriting. "This looks like fountain pen ink to me."

He held the note up for her to examine and she dipped her head in agreement. "It does. I hadn't noticed that."

Robbie held the note up to the light to confirm it to himself, seeing the slight changes in how the ink lay on the paper. Too irregular for either a ballpoint or gel ink pen.

"Definitely fountain pen, and if we can get a fingerprint, match the ink's profile with one at your stalker's location—"

"And your assailant. He hit you," she said and surprised him by tenderly running her fingers along the bruised area on his cheek.

Robbie nodded and added, "The two things will help but we'll also have to get a handwriting match. Which means dinner again at Alberto's to get a sample of Bart's."

Selene worried her lower lip again and her hesitation was clear. "Is that necessary? Why do you think it might be him?"

With a big shrug, Robbie said, "He rubbed me the wrong way but a fingerprint on the paper alone isn't enough to prove he's the one who wrote them. He might have just touched the notes somehow. That's why we need the writing sample."

Selene sipped her tea, hands wrapped around the mug as she considered all he'd said. With a jerk of her head, she said, "Whatever you need."

What he needed, more than anything, was for her to give him as much information as she could. But he tempered that need with awareness of all she'd suffered in her short life. He had to be gentle.

"Are you okay with me looking through these while you tell me about the first one you got?"

"Sure," she said and took another sip of her tea. She laid her mug on the table with shaky hands and then spread her fingers wide as if that could give her stability by rooting her to the tabletop.

"I kept the first one because it was a little flattering to get a fan note. I did the same with the next two and then something started to feel off, so I threw them all out," she admitted.

"Did anyone else see those first notes? Or see you tossing them?" he said, wondering if it was someone at the bar who might be the possible stalker.

An emphatic nod was followed by, "I showed the first note to the manager, just kind of in passing. It was…flattering at first. It had been so long since…"

She didn't need to finish, and his heart ached at the pain she had suffered.

He gingerly slipped his hand over hers and once again she

surprised him by turning her hand and holding his. "When our first security program took off, I loved seeing the positive reviews. It was a high to have someone recognize what we'd done," he admitted.

Her lips tilted up in a lopsided smile. "It did feel amazing but then it didn't and now... I want it to stop."

He squeezed her hand in reassurance. "We *will* stop him. Come the morning I'll get Sophie, Ryder and the SBS team working on this."

The half grin broadened into a full-lipped smile and her eyes lost some of their hurt. "That would be great. But we need to let them know not to bother Rhea and Jax," she reminded.

With another gentle clasp of her hand, he said, "We will. In the meantime, I'd like to go to your performance tomorrow. Maybe check out the location and speak to the manager. Are you okay with that?"

"I'd love for you to see me perform but I don't want to cause the bar any trouble," she said, worry slipping back over her features.

"I understand and I won't cause any problems. I promise," he said and did a little cross over his heart in emphasis.

"I'd appreciate that," she said with a dip of her head.

"I understand you don't work on the days you perform," he said, recalling something that Rhea had once mentioned during an earlier visit to his cousin Jackson.

"I have Fridays and weekends off. I like to take time to prepare," she said with a nod.

"Great. I hope you don't mind doing a little something with me tomorrow," he said with a smile and playful shake of their joined hands.

"Why does that grin make me think you want to do something adventurous?" she asked, eyes narrowed as she considered him.

"I do. We're going to the shelter to find you a dog."

SELENE'S MIND WAS in overdrive with the sounds and sights of all the animals and visitors at the shelter.

Young children excitedly darted from cage to cage in search of a new pet while their parents followed along indulgently, trying to steer them toward their preferred choice.

Balls of fur in all sizes, shapes and colors yipped, yapped or meowed for attention or skittered away from an overeager patron at the cage doors.

Robbie seemed to sense her overload since he tucked his hand into hers, squeezed it and did a little teasing shake. "It's a little much, isn't it?" he said, reading her mind.

"It is. The puppies are so cute but I'm not sure I have the time to train one," she said while at the same time laughing at the antics of one adorable tan and brown poodle mix in a nearby cage.

The puppy's excited yips and jumping drew her attention but then another sight captured it and had her walking to a nearby cage.

She squatted to stare at the sad-looking dog who lay there and eyed her with a doleful dark gaze. The sadness touched her since she'd seen it in her own eyes as she stared into a mirror and asked herself "Why?"

"Poor thing," she said and steadied herself by gripping the cage wires.

The dog, a white and gray pit bull mix, lumbered over to the cage door and licked Selene's fingers, yanking a laugh from her.

"You're a good pup," she said and slipped her fingers through the cage to stroke the dog's short, smooth fur coat.

The dog whined and snuggled closer, eager for the love.

Robbie sidled closer to them and said, "Her name's Lily. She's a two-year-old pit bull/Staffordshire bull terrier mix."

"She's so friendly," Selene said and peered up at him, wondering what he was thinking about the older dog.

One of the shelter workers, sensing their interest, approached them and said, "It's tough to place dogs that are part pit bull, but Lily is quite gentle and very well trained. She belonged to a young police officer who was killed on duty and his father took her in, but she was too active for him."

As if to prove her comment about being well trained, the shelter worker leashed Lily, took her out of the cage and then ran her through several commands.

The dog responded immediately to all of them and the worker, a young woman, handed Selene the leash. "Why don't you try?"

Selene hesitated but then grabbed the leash and said, "Sit."

Lily immediately reacted by sitting on her haunches and looking up at Selene, as if waiting for another command.

Selene held out her hand and said, "Give me your paw."

As she had before, Lily immediately complied, earning a head rub from Selene. Obviously happy, Lily lay down and exposed her belly for a rub and Selene gleefully responded, stroking her hand across the pale fur on her belly.

"SHE TRUSTS YOU. That's a good sign," Robbie said, watching as Lily and Selene interacted.

Selene peered up at him. "I know you mentioned getting a puppy, but Lily is already trained and she seemed so sad when we first saw her but look at her now," Selene gushed in a flood of words.

Lily was happy and not having to train a puppy was a good thing. Plus, Lily might make a good guard dog with some additional instruction. Last but not least, Selene and Lily seemed to have bonded.

"I think she's a great choice. Our K-9 trainer Sara Hernandez might even be able to help us train Lily to do some other things," Robbie said and glanced at the young woman from the shelter. "What do we need to do to take Lily home?"

Chapter Seven

Robbie walked beside Selene as she held Lily's leash on the way back to the condo after picking up pet supplies at a local store.

The dog almost skipped ahead of them, a jaunty grin on her face, a brand-new collar with her dog license and a tag with her address jangling almost happily.

Lily had been quite obedient in the shop, almost docile when a smaller dog had started barking at her. Lily had responded by grabbing the leash and pulling Selene away from the annoying little chihuahua.

A good sign, Robbie thought as he turned his attention to the streets around them, vigilant for anything untoward.

As they neared an alley close to the condo, which is where he suspected his assailant had hidden the night he'd gotten punched, he slowed and peered toward the space between the buildings.

No one, luckily, but then Lily's sharp bark drew his attention back to the street.

Selene stopped and Lily sat at her feet, staring up at Bart as he walked toward them.

The other man had been smiling until he spotted the dog. His smile grew brittle then as he slowed to stand before them.

"Nice to see you, Selene," he said and barely glanced at Robbie, ignoring him to stare down at Lily.

"Dog-sitting?" he asked, almost too hopefully.

"No, I just adopted her. Isn't she cute?" Selene said and bent to rub the pittie's head.

He was sure Bart wasn't thinking that Lily was cute. If he was the stalker, and his gut was telling him that was a distinct possibility, the last thing he wanted was a dog as powerful as Lily protecting Selene.

"She's very pretty," he said and also bent to pet her, but Lily did a little warning growl, upset about the invasion of her space.

Bart immediately drew his hand back. "Not very friendly."

"They say dogs are a good judge of character," Robbie said and rubbed the dog's head, earning a friendly lick of his hand.

"Obviously not," Bart challenged and pulled his shoulders back in a move intended to make him look bigger by pushing out his well-muscled chest.

While Bart was about his height but thicker with muscle, Robbie didn't doubt he could win a fight if need be. But now wasn't the time for that. Instead, he asked, "What brings you around here?"

"On my way to work and thought I'd drop by the shop and say hi, but then I remembered Selene has a show tonight," Bart replied. He tried to pet Lily again, earning another low growl.

It bothered Robbie that Bart seemed to know Selene's schedule so well. If he did and he wasn't the stalker, was the stalker as familiar with Selene's habits?

"I guess you should get to work then. Wouldn't want to be late," Robbie pressed, peered at Selene and added, "We need to get going too, right?"

"We do. Lily needs to get acquainted with her new home and we'll need to walk her before the show," Selene said and offered Bart a hesitant smile. "I hope you don't mind."

Bart waved off her concerns with his hands. "Of course not. Hopefully, I'll see you soon."

With a glare in Robbie's direction, Bart stalked off.

"Testosterone. Again," Selene said with a tinkling laugh that drew a happy hop and bark from Lily.

"Like I said before, he rubs me the wrong way and Lily didn't like him either," Robbie said as they walked the final yards to the building and then headed to Rhea's condo.

Lily balked at entering at first, but Selene cajoled her into her new home and showed her around while Robbie placed the bags with the pet supplies on the dining table. The dog's new bed had been too bulky to carry, and the pet store would deliver it well before the time for them to leave for Selene's show.

Which reminded him that Sophie and Ryder should be arriving soon so that they could have a video conference with the Miami team at South Beach Security.

He quickly got to work on finding a spot to set out bowls with food and water for Lily and tucked the fresh food into the fridge and the kibble into one of the cabinets.

Selene sashayed out of the hallway, Lily in the lead, and as they neared him, she unclipped the leash to let Lily roam around on her own. At a hall tree by the front door, she hung up the leash and then approached him.

"Thank you," she said and surprised him with a hug.

"What for?" he asked, although he could guess.

"For finding Lily. I think she'll be good for me. I find it hard to be alone sometimes," she admitted. But buried in there was maybe something else, namely that she'd be alone once he returned to Miami.

With a quick shrug, he said, "She will be good company and more importantly, a good protector, I think."

Almost as if to prove it, Lily barked and jumped to her feet as the ring of the intercom warned someone was at the building door.

"Sit, Lily. Quiet," Robbie said, and the dog immediately obeyed.

Selene walked to the intercom and after checking that it was Sophie and Ryder, buzzed open the door.

She waited for them there and Lily started barking and came to Selene's side as her sharper dog hearing picked up on activity in the hall.

"Sit, Lily," Selene said, and the pittie obeyed, but as Selene opened the door, Robbie had to grab Lily's collar as the dog rushed toward their guests.

But the pittie immediately quieted at Robbie's command.

His sister Sophie arched a manicured brow and said, "You got a dog?"

She held her hand out and Robbie released Lily so she could scent Sophie's hand.

With a welcoming lick, Lily accepted Sophie but then sat and peered up at Ryder and Delilah, the corgi sitting at his side.

The two dogs stared at each other as if sizing each other up, and then tentatively approached, Delilah almost crawling over on her short legs. They met, nose to nose, Lily clearly in a dominant position, but then the two gamboled playfully before trotting away to sit together by one of the sofas.

Relieved, Robbie hugged his sister and shook Ryder's hand. "Glad to have you here."

"Glad to help in any way that we can," Ryder said and glanced in Selene's direction.

"I'll get the notes," Selene said and rushed off to her bedroom for the jewelry box.

Sophie narrowed her gaze and skipped it across his face. "It looks painful and, por favor, don't tell me the other guy looks worse," she said and gingerly ran her hand across his bruised cheek.

"Not as sore now and the black eye gives me a dangerous look, don't you think?" he said, trying to downplay his injuries.

"A ridiculous look," she said, her voice tight with emotion, and hugged him hard again.

Their buzzing phones warned that the time for niceties was over, and they had to get to work.

Robbie hurried away to power up his laptop and get the video feed displaying on the large TV screen on the central wall of the room.

Sophie, Ryder and he sat at the table and, seconds later, Selene placed the jewelry box in front of Sophie and Ryder.

Ryder opened the box and peered inside but didn't remove the notes there.

He glanced at Robbie. "Did you touch these?"

Robbie waved off Ryder's worry. "With white gloves on to avoid any transference of DNA or prints."

Ryder nodded. "Good. I'll take this in and have our CSI team see what they can get."

The ringtones of the video call software warned the SBS team was ready to join them and with a few keystrokes, their faces popped up on the TV.

SELENE SAT NEXT to Robbie as he introduced her to his Miami cousins.

"Selene, meet Trey, Mia, and Ricky. Trey is the acting head of the agency now. Mia joined the agency about a year ago after being a successful lifestyle influencer, and Ricky is a psychologist who assists when he can," Robbie said and his pride and love for his family was evident in the tone of his voice.

"I'm happy to meet you," she said and after a quick glance at Robbie, added, "I just wish it wasn't under these circumstances."

"We wish the same and hope you and Ryder will be able to visit with us in Miami," Mia immediately responded, a bright smile on her face.

"We hope so too," Ryder said and looked lovingly at Sophie.

Trey, ever the leader and head cop, said, "In the meantime, can you fill us in on what's happening and who gave you that shiner?" He emphasized his question by circling an index finger as if highlighting Robbie's black eye.

Robbie provided a quick report on everything they had so far and what Ryder's CBI people would be doing. He also made some suggestions on how to improve security at the studio, gallery and condo and what Sophie and he could do.

Selene's mind reeled with the many cameras that Robbie wanted to install and what that might cost. She waved her hands in the air to stop him and said, "I'm not sure I can afford all those upgrades—not to mention the work you, your sister and your cousins will do."

Robbie took hold of her hand and squeezed. "You don't need to worry about that."

On camera, Ricky's gaze seemed to shift to that gesture and then to Robbie. As one of the dogs barked, Ricky's gaze widened even more and he said, "Is that a dog I hear?"

Robbie nodded. "Two, actually. Ryder has a corgi and Selene and I rescued a pittie mix this morning. It'll be good for Selene to have company and the added protection."

Ricky dipped his head in acknowledgement, and something seemed to pass between the two men that warned Selene that they had discussed her. But she'd take that up with Robbie later.

"It sounds like you have things under control, but we can search for those CCTV cameras in the area if that will help Sophie and you with whatever else you need to do," Trey said and glanced at Mia who added, "I'm sure John can assist with the CCTV search."

Her billionaire tech husband probably had programs and personnel to help with that kind of work, Selene thought, grateful that she had Robbie and the rest of the South Beach Security team on her side.

"That sounds great, Trey. We'd really like to focus on evidence gathering and improving the security around here," Sophie said, and Robbie echoed her comment.

"I'd like to start at the gallery and condo if we can get the equipment by tomorrow," Robbie said.

"I can connect you with local suppliers that CBI uses and anything else you need," Ryder added and slipped an arm around Sophie's shoulders in a gesture of support.

"Gracias, Ryder. That will be a big help," Sophie said and brushed a kiss across his cheek.

"Yes, gracias," Robbie said and turned his attention to her. "I should have asked before, but are you okay with all this?"

For years she'd let her husband steamroll her and then her captors in the months she'd been imprisoned after being kidnapped. She appreciated that Robbie was giving her some control, some choice, about what happened. But it also made her remember that look he'd shared with his cousin Ricky, making her wonder if they'd discussed her.

"I'm okay with this if Rhea is. It's her gallery and condo. Jason at the studio as well, I guess," she said with a shrug.

"What about the bar?" Sophie asked and jotted down some notes on a pad she had pulled out.

"I think they already have cameras," Selene said, recalling the various signs about video recording at the bar.

"I can confirm tonight when I go to the show with Selene. I want to check out backstage also," Robbie said and quickly tacked on, "If that's okay with you, Selene."

While she appreciated his consideration, it bothered her as well that he viewed her as so fragile to require his coddling. "You don't need to ask my permission, Robbie," she said, sharply enough that everyone's eyebrows shot up around the table.

Instantly contrite, she waved her hands in apology and blew out a frustrated sigh. "I'm sorry. I didn't mean to snap."

Robbie seemed ready to say "It's okay" but stopped himself. After a deep, bracing breath, he glanced at Sophie and Ryder and said, "Do you want to come with us tonight?"

Sophie and Ryder shared a look before Ryder held up the jewelry box. "I was hoping to get this to our lab and then get Sophie settled at my place."

"And while I know John Wilson can search for those CCTV cameras, I'd like to work on it myself as well. Maybe walk around with Ryder and get the lay of the land," Sophie advised.

Robbie nodded. "Good. I can send you the addresses of the studio and bar. I'd also like you to keep an eye on the restaurant. Alberto's. It's one of Selene's faves."

"Got it," Sophie said and wrote down the restaurant name on her pad.

"I guess we're all set and should let Selene get some rest before it's time for her performance," Robbie said, ever considerate.

As it had before, it roused unreasonable anger that Selene tamped down as Sophie and Ryder packed up and headed out the door.

When Robbie closed the door behind them, he faced her and laid his arms across his chest. "Let it out. I can tell you're angry at me."

The words erupted from her with unexpected force. "I'm not some fragile flower that can't handle things. Heck, I've survived more in my life than most could imagine."

ROBBIE UNDERSTOOD THAT more than most since he'd reviewed the files on her kidnapping.

Hands held out in pleading, he said, "I'm just trying to be understanding."

She arched a brow, and her blue eyes were filled with icy anger as she said, "Is that why you discussed me with Ricky?"

Embarrassed heat flooded his face at being found out, although he'd do it all over again if he had to. "I saw how you pulled away sometimes. That you were uncomfortable. I didn't want to do anything that might make you uneasy, so I spoke to Ricky since he works with women who've been abused."

Selene tucked her arms tight around herself and the shimmer of tears replaced her earlier anger. Voice tight, she said, "I don't want to feel like…like you're analyzing me when we're together. That you're afraid of me being afraid and we're both afraid of whatever this is we're feeling."

He muttered a curse beneath his breath, shook his head and then approached her cautiously, as afraid as she had said. He gently cupped her cheek and was grateful when she didn't pull away. Sadly, he said, "What I'm afraid of the most is that we won't get to explore whatever this is that we're feeling."

A tear escaped and rolled down her cheek and he tenderly swiped it away with his thumb, dragging a small smile from her. "I wish things could be different. Easier. I know you want to treat me with kid gloves but the greatest gift you could give me is just to treat me like any other woman you want to date."

He took a moment to digest that request combined with the recommendations Ricky had made. Selene's request won out.

Inching closer, until her warm breath gusted across his face and her blue eyes widened in surprise, he said, "What I would want from a woman I dated, a beautiful and intelligent woman like you, is a kiss."

He brushed that kiss across her lips, the touch so light and brief it seemed to take her a moment to realize he'd done it.

But then she nodded and backed away, her surprise giving way to acceptance and the barest hint of a smile. "Okay. That's okay," she stammered as if in shock.

He arched a brow and grinned. "Only okay? I'll have to try harder next time."

She chuckled, shook her head and—eyes bright—she said, "Yes, you will."

Chapter Eight

Selene walked in through the performer's entrance in the alley behind the bar, Robbie trailing behind her.

She'd never thought anything about it before, but now it made her uneasy that she had to go down the relatively dark, narrow alley. The only illumination came from a streetlight that cast its glow at the entrance of the alley and a single dim bulb by the bar's back door.

Entering, she encountered the head of security who split his time between walking around backstage and the restaurant area and keeping an eye on the guards at the front door.

"Evening, Ralph."

"Good to see you, Selene," he said and eyeballed Robbie. "He with you?"

"Yes, he is. Robbie, meet Ralph. He's the head of security for the bar," Selene said and gestured to the older, brawny man.

Robbie shook Ralph's hand. "Nice to meet you. Are you watching this back door?"

Ralph shook his head, and his brow furrowed as he examined Robbie. "Just making my rounds. You a cop or something?"

"A friend, but Selene's gotten some not-so-nice notes backstage," he said, obviously wanting not to upset the other man.

Ralph's eyes opened wide, and he stared hard at Selene. "Is that true? Why didn't you say something?"

Selene bit her lower lip and then blurted out, "I didn't want to cause a problem."

Ralph tapped his broad, muscled chest and said, "It's a problem with me if someone's bothering you."

"Glad to hear that," Robbie said and immediately pushed on. "Would you mind if I take a look around at your security and camera feeds? Maybe get access to them," he said, then took out his wallet and handed the man his business card.

Ralph eyeballed the card in his large, calloused hands and then eyeballed Robbie. "South Beach Security. You're kinda far from home, aren't you?"

"Visiting family in Regina, and who knows? Maybe we'll open a Colorado branch so we can spend more time here," Robbie said with an easygoing smile and peek in her direction.

Ralph's gaze skipped from Robbie to her. Tucking the card into the pocket of his leather vest, he said, "Whatever you need to keep Selene safe. I can show you around whenever you want, and I'll text you a link and log-in info to access the camera feeds."

"Why not now? I'd like to get ready for the show," Selene said and gestured to the tight hallway. "The greenroom is just right there—down from the security area."

"We'll walk you there and then I'll show Robbie what we've got," Ralph said and brushed past them to lead the way.

Sandwiched between the two men, one large and thick and looking a lot like a rough biker and Robbie, who was all lean, strong muscle, and kind of hipster, Selene felt safe.

At the door to the small greenroom, she hesitated and looked around for one of the luxurious envelopes that held such vile words.

Nothing, she thought with a sigh of relief.

Robbie laid a gentle hand at her waist, leaned close and whispered against her ear, "You okay?"

She smiled and nodded. "I am. Thanks."

"Good," he said, skimmed a kiss across her cheek and followed Ralph to the security office, which was no more than about ten feet down the hall.

Relieved, Selene strolled over to the small couch whose stained cushions sagged from the weight of the many performers who had sat there while waiting for the call.

Most times it was just the call to hit the stage to perform. For the luckier ones, it was the call to move up to better things.

Like the call she was hoping for from the Miami producer who was interested in her work.

She just had to record one more song and she'd have a good sample to send off to see if the producer would want to sign her. The producer was a woman who'd made it big with a mix of Latin singers, urban rappers and country music artists with crossover appeal.

Selene hoped she could fit in somewhere in that eclectic mix—much like she fit in at the bar, which started the night out with her more lyrical, uplifting songs but sometimes ended the night with heavy metal, rappers or electronic dance music.

She laid her guitar case on the couch beside the other case there. She recognized it as belonging to Rachel, the guitarist in her backup band. Slipping out of her jacket, she tossed it next to the other clothing there. Her drummer Adam's denim jacket was negligently tossed across the top of the couch, beside Sam and Monty's hoodies. She opened her guitar case and took out her instrument.

Walking with her guitar and purse to the seats positioned before a long counter space in front of bright lights and mirrors, she sat, laid her purse on the counter and took a moment to tune the guitar. Satisfied, she set it beside her and stared at herself in the mirror. Presentable enough, but she took a brush and some makeup out of her purse and did a final tweak. She added a little more blush and another swipe of a lip stain in a deeper red since the bright stage lights could sometimes wash out her color.

But as she swiped, she caught sight of someone at her door, hoodie pulled up to hide their face.

She shot to her feet and whirled around, but the figure had moved on.

Or did I just imagine it? she thought, heart racing so hard she had to lay a hand there to quiet it.

But relief flooded her as Robbie poked his head in a heartbeat later. Worry slipped into his gaze as he saw her, walked over and tenderly took hold of her hands. "Everything okay?"

She nodded. "I thought I saw someone at the door."

He looked back in that direction and shook his head. "I didn't pass anyone on my way."

She dipped her head. "Probably just my imagination."

"Understandable," he said and stroked a hand across her hair. "Ralph is going to give me access to whatever CCTV recordings he has. Hopefully, we'll find something on there."

"Hopefully," she said just as one of the stagehands came to the door, held one hand up—fingers outspread—and said, "Five minutes, Selene."

"Thanks, Scott. I'll be there in a second," she said. She breathed in a deep inhale and then released it in a rush.

He brushed back a lock of her hair, skimmed a kiss on her cheek and whispered, "Break a leg."

She smiled, appreciating not only his presence but also that he was no longer treating her like a delicate china doll.

"Thank you. For everything."

He pointed a finger toward the door. "I'll follow you to the wings."

Selene grabbed her guitar in one hand and his hand in the other, pulling him the short distance past the security office to the darkened edges of the stage where a few men and another woman waited.

She greeted them all and introduced them to Robbie. "Meet Adam, Monty, Sam and Rachel. They're my backup band."

"Nice to meet you," Robbie said and shook all their hands, but something told Selene that he was also getting a read on them. She didn't doubt he'd be asking for their full names later to check them out.

Scott approached, hand raised with two fingers held up. "Two minutes."

Selene skipped her gaze across her fellow musicians and nodded. "We're ready."

Robbie waited in the wings while the bar owner introduced Selene and the band. A round of loud applause erupted, pleasing him.

Selene and the other musicians were clearly well liked.

He lingered there, getting a feel for the area and the backstage activity as stagehand Scott scurried down the hall and Ralph did another walk through the space.

Since he wanted to see for himself what the entire backstage area was like, he did his own inspection, moving back toward the greenroom. It was empty and he closed the door to secure Selene's things.

He pushed toward the back door and realized that there was a unisex bathroom right by the door and then another tight hall to his right. Strolling down that corridor, he noticed it led to the wings on the other side of the small stage. It was quieter there and as he stood there for long minutes, watching Selene perform, he realized that no one seemed to walk through that area, including Ralph.

At one point Selene saw him there and smiled so beautifully and full of happiness that it made his heart skip a beat.

She was in her element, doing what she loved, and it showed.

Which only made him even more determined to safeguard her and her dream.

He hurried back to the main corridor and the beehive of backstage activity. Ralph and Scott were hard at work. The guard in the security office was monitoring a dozen cameras located at various spots both inside and outside of the bar.

Satisfied, although he intended to speak to Ralph about the stage left wings, he hurried down the steps to the right of the stage, walked into the main area of the bar and then slipped to a far wall to get a sense of the space.

Directly before the stage was a small area where patrons could stand to hear the show. After that, lines of tables that could seat four filled the central portion of the area. Beyond them were high-top tables for two where patrons could either stand or sit to view the show. Flanking both sides of the tables were long narrow bars lined with stools.

Virtually all the seats were full. Waiters and waitresses flitted here and there, taking and filling food and drink orders. It made him wonder where the kitchen was located and who had access to it.

The motion of the curtains along stage left snared his attention.

Was someone there?

Selene must have seen someone also since she stumbled for a second before returning to the performance. But the tension was evident in the way she shifted on her stool and set her gaze in that direction.

Worried, Robbie hurried backstage and rushed to the wings on stage left but no one was there.

As she had before, Selene noticed his presence there and the release of her tension was visible. Her shoulders loosened and she gave herself over to her music, body moving in emphasis of the words and notes spilling from her guitar and the instruments of her band members.

He lingered there, examining the space. Had he imagined

the hooded shadow he'd seen there? But he negated that doubt. Selene had seen someone as well.

Backtracking, he searched for any other entrance to the area but with no luck.

Still, he didn't want to take a chance and remained there, viewing the performance until Selene finished and the bar owner came out to give his spiel about the night's specials on drinks and food.

Since Selene and her band were heading for stage right, he hurried toward the greenroom and met them there as they entered and moved aside guitar cases to sit on the couch and on the stools at the counter.

"You were great," Robbie said and hugged a slightly sweaty Selene. "You were all great," he added, skipping his gaze across all the musicians.

"Thank you," Selene said, and her bandmates echoed the thanks as they drank water from bottles someone had set out while they were performing.

Scott maybe? he thought, assuming it might be one of his duties as a stagehand.

"Do you have another set to do?" he asked, unfamiliar with her routine.

She held up an index finger. "One more and then we usually grab a bite in the bar."

"Part of the perks of the job," Rachel said with a roll of deep brown eyes heavily accented with eyeliner. She had more of a goth look about her while the other bandmates screamed grunge or alternative rock.

"I'll take anything that puts food in my belly," Adam said playfully and rubbed a stomach starting to show a little bit of paunch. Maybe he was older or just looked older since he was balding slightly.

Monty and Sam laughed, almost in unison, and now that

he had more time to scrutinize them, he realized how much they looked alike.

"You guys twins?" he asked, trying to confirm it.

"We are, but not identical like Rhea and Selene," Monty began and Sam ended it with, "Fraternal."

"Cool," he said, taking in the slight differences in coloring and facial features of the two.

"Ten," Scott called out as he whizzed by the door.

"I don't know about you, but I need a bathroom break," Adam said and bounded out the door, followed by the two other men.

Rachel and Selene lingered, sipping their waters and not really talking which warned that maybe not all was right between the two women.

But as the men returned, Selene said, "Do you need to go?"

With a nod, Rachel joined Selene as the two women left and he hung back, wanting to question the men.

"Have you guys seen anything unusual backstage?" he asked.

The three men looked at each other and the assortment of shrugs and head shakes offered an answer.

"Nothing. Why?" Adam asked and pitched his empty bottle into a nearby wastebasket.

"Selene got some notes that upset her. You haven't seen anything?" he pressed again.

Monty and Sam shared a look before Monty said, "She showed us a note a couple of weeks ago, but she seemed excited about it."

"I think it was a fan letter," Sam added with a nonchalant shrug.

Rachel and Selene returned at that moment and Robbie decided not to raise the issue in front of the other woman. Call it intuition but his gut was saying there was more to Rachel that he needed to know before involving her in the investigation.

"Five," Scott said and stood at the door holding up five fingers.

"Got it," Adam called out and looked at all his bandmates. "You all ready?"

"We're good," Monty said, speaking for the two brothers.

"I just need to freshen up," Rachel said and hurried to the mirrors and a large black purse on the counter.

"I'm ready," Selene said and with that, she and the other band members hurried to the wings.

As Selene stood there, Robbie whispered in her ear, "I'll be at stage left so don't worry about a thing."

She nodded and smiled. A second later, she brushed that smile across his cheek in a kiss. "Lord, I've marked you," she said and ran a thumb across his cheek to remove the red stain from her kiss.

"I don't mind," he said and dropped a quick kiss on her lips before hurrying away.

As he passed the door to the greenroom, he realized Rachel was still there, applying eyeliner. Her dark gaze met his in the mirror, almost challenging.

"Two minutes," Scott called out to her as he rushed past, nearly knocking Robbie into the wall.

Robbie didn't wait for Rachel to exit the room. He hurried to the other corridor and the wings there, but hid deep in the shadows, hoping to surprise anyone who might find a way to stand there.

No one appeared for the entire length of the performance.

Either Selene and he had imagined it or the person had decided to stay away, either because they were done stalking for the night or because they realized they'd been seen. Or maybe, and he considered it an unlikely possibility, it had just been someone watching the show with no harm intended.

When the bar owner emerged from the bar floor once again

to announce the next performers, Selene and her band members hurried off.

He rushed to the greenroom to find it a hive of activity as the other performers had arrived and were preparing for their gig.

While Selene and her band members gathered their things, the other band tossed jackets, guitar cases and other items onto the couch and counter. It confirmed to Robbie how difficult it might be to get any evidence from this area because of the high traffic in and out of it.

He took hold of Selene's guitar case as she jerked her purse over her shoulder and slipped his hand into hers to lead her down the hall to the main area of the bar. The owner had kindly reserved a table for the performers at the very back of the space and close to a door that he now realized led to a kitchen.

As they all sat around the table, a waiter came over and said, "The usual?"

Everyone murmured their agreement, and the older man peered at him. "What about you?"

"What's the usual?" he asked, skipping his gaze to Selene and the other band members.

"Burgers, fries and the daily special IPA. It's the best bet," Selene said with a soft smile.

He nodded. "The usual for me too."

The waiter hurried away, and Selene and the others started chatting about the sets they'd done that night.

Robbie sat back, taking in the interactions between the musicians to get a read on them.

As he'd sensed before, Adam seemed to be viewed as an elder statesman by all, possibly because he was older and had been playing the bar scene for far longer than the rest.

Monty and Sam were lively and funny and their habit of

finishing each other's sentences almost made them seem like a comedy team.

Rachel, he examined as the conversation continued. She was older than he'd first thought. The heavier makeup she wore onstage hid some of the lines around her eyes and mouth. He couldn't call them laugh lines because he hadn't seen her break even a small smile or chuckle the entire time, even with the twins' antics.

That made him wonder if Rachel resented that a younger, seemingly more talented woman, was now the center of attention.

His thoughts were interrupted by the arrival of a duo of busboys with their meals and beers, and silence quickly ensued as hunger took over.

Beside him, Selene dug into the large burger with gusto, and he did the same, enjoying what was a surprisingly tasty half pound of sirloin, if he had to guess, tucked into a yeasty roll and topped with a special sauce with a little zing of spice.

"Delicious," he murmured around a mouthful of burger and bun.

"Kelly makes a great burger," Adam said and as if to prove his point, bit off a big piece of his.

The others around the table echoed his statement and turned their attention to the meals, but after a few minutes, the conversation resumed.

"Are you almost done with your recordings for that producer?" Rachel asked, then stuffed a fry into her mouth.

"Almost. Just one more song that we hope to record tomorrow," Selene said. She picked up her beer and took a dainty sip that left her with a partial beer mustache.

He made a motion with his index finger across his lips and Selene laughed, grabbed a napkin and wiped it off.

"Which song is that?" Adam asked.

"'Wait for you,'" Selene said, and it seemed to him that

he'd heard a beautiful ballad with a similar chorus during to-night's sets.

"Good choice," Monty said, and Sam and Adam agreed.

"That's about your speed," Rachel said with a slight twist of her lips.

SELENE TENSED AT the other woman's snub, but she didn't take the bait.

"Thanks, I think it is," she said, earning a more obvious sneer from Rachel.

She didn't know why the other woman continued to dislike her. They'd been working together for nearly a year now and Selene had always gone out of her way to be nice and to let Rachel be front and center on some of their duets.

Nothing seemed to be enough, but she tried not to let Rachel bother her. Only it did and her appetite fled. She took the last bite of her burger and trailed her fries through her ketchup mindlessly as her band members launched into a discussion about her possibly being signed by the Miami producer.

Robbie slipped an arm around her shoulders, hugged her and bent his head close. "It's been a long day. You must be tired," he whispered.

She nodded. "I am. If you're done, I'd like to go."

"I'm done," he said and shot to his feet. Facing her band members, he added, "Time to go."

Selene rose and as they shifted their chairs back to leave the table, her purse slipped off her chair and landed on the floor, and some of the contents spilled out.

Her breath caught in her chest as she noticed the envelope in the high-end stationery favored by her stalker.

Chapter Nine

Robbie snatched an arm around Selene's waist as her knees buckled.

He helped her back into the chair and was about to ask her what was wrong when something bright and rectangular on the floor snared his attention.

Another note, delivered right under their noses.

Selene reached for it, but he blocked her hand to stop her. "Leave it to me."

He grabbed his napkin from the table, picked up the note and wrapped it in the napkin. The napkin might have his DNA on it, and possibly that of a server, but it was all he had to protect the evidence.

Adam was quick to ask, "What's wrong, Selene? You look like death warmed over."

"It's nothing," she said shakily and locked her gaze with his as if seeking his permission to say more.

He hesitated, aware that those around the table had had access to Selene's purse while in the greenroom. But maybe it was time to press them and see their reactions.

Holding up the napkin with the envelope, he said, "Someone has been sending threatening notes to Selene. They also attacked me the other night."

As he peered at the men, he sized them up again and

thought that they all could have fit the general description of the assailant.

"My team and I are investigating. The men knew about some earlier notes, but what about you?" he said and trained his gaze on Rachel.

She pointed a black nail-polished finger at her chest and said, "Don't look at me."

But he did, thinking that of all of them, she might have the best reason to hate Selene.

At his prolonged stare, she jumped to her feet, nearly knocking her chair over with the sudden movement.

"I don't need this," Rachel said and stalked out of the bar.

She was tall for a woman but whip thin. Maybe not the right build for his attacker but then again, it had happened suddenly, and it was always possible she had an accomplice.

"You should have said something about them getting nasty," Adam said, accusation alive in his voice.

"I didn't know what to do about them," Selene said, hands held out in pleading.

The three men looked at each other, and then all nodded in unison, as in sync with each other as they were up on the stage.

"We have your back," Monty said.

"Whatever you need," Sam echoed.

"You should have told us," Adam repeated, but then wagged his head and added, "You can count on us."

SELENE APPRECIATED THEIR SUPPORT, but it didn't make it any easier.

Even with Robbie at her side, someone had managed to leave her a nastygram. She didn't doubt the note contained another threat.

"Anything you can remember about tonight that might be unusual would be a good start," Robbie said, then pulled out his wallet and handed each of the men his business card.

As they nodded, Robbie stood and offered her a hand to steady her.

She rose, but then bent and hastily stuffed the spilled contents of her purse back into her bag.

They made a quick exit out of the bar and turned toward home, silent for long minutes. Robbie's pace was hurried, forcing Selene to almost take two steps to his one until she tugged on his hand, urging him to slow down.

"I'm sorry. I just want to get home and take Lily for a walk. She's probably—"

He stopped as his phone pinged to alert him of an incoming message.

Glancing at it, a tight smile erupted on his face. "Ralph did as promised and gave me access. I'll check the camera feeds as soon as we're home and hopefully, there will be something there that might give us a clue as to who did this."

"That's good to know," she said, feeling better about it and surprisingly, feeling something warm and fuzzy every time he said the word *home*.

She told herself not to read too much into it as they resumed their walk, at a more comfortable pace. Lots of people probably called where they were staying for the moment *home*.

She'd even called the place where she had lived with her abusive husband home—not that it really felt like it at the end. But for a little while, it had felt that way.

But her parents had always provided Rhea and her a loving and supportive environment until their untimely deaths in a car crash a few years earlier.

It made her swing his hand almost playfully, even though that was the last thing that she should be feeling considering what had just happened.

But having him there provided a big measure of comfort she'd never felt with any men other than her father, Robbie's cousin Jackson and Jackson's father. They'd always been the kind of strong, stalwart men you knew you could count on. And although Robbie struck her as more of a gamer than a cowboy or warrior, she didn't doubt she could count on him as well.

She buzzed them in at the condo and in no time, they were in Rhea's apartment. Lily excitedly raced over, happy to see them.

Selene bent and rubbed the dog's head and body, earning a series of doggy kisses that had her laughing.

"Let's take her for a quick walk," Robbie said, and they headed back out.

Lily tugged on her leash, racing ahead of them into the elevator and out of the lobby onto the street. They had barely gone a block when she relieved herself.

They picked up and continued around the block so the pittie could get some exercise before returning to Rhea's condo.

Robbie almost ran to his knapsack to haul out his laptop to get to work when they returned.

Since she suspected he intended to put in a long night to ascertain who had left tonight's note and how they'd done it, she hustled to the kitchen to make a pot of coffee. The simple act of filling the coffeemaker and counting out the scoops of coffee was the kind of mindless task that pulled her mind away from what had happened that night.

Not wanting to interrupt Robbie, who had also called Sophie and Ryder about the new note, she dillydallied in the kitchen, grabbing mugs and spoons from the cabinets. She pulled the half-and-half from the fridge and waited until enough coffee had dripped into the pot to make a mug of coffee for Robbie.

As she did so, Lily followed her around, staying close. As Robbie had hoped, the dog's presence brought a level of comfort, security and companionship.

She added several spoons of sugar and a good amount of

half-and-half to Robbie's mug, remembering that he liked it sweet and light.

Cradling the warm mug in two hands, she walked it over to the table and set it down, earning a mouthed "Thank you."

"You're welcome," she mouthed back and returned to the kitchen to make herself a mug, Lily tagging along.

If Robbie was going to be staying up, so was she—even if she'd be tired for the next day's recording session.

Thinking of the recording session, it reminded her of Rachel's comment that had rankled her earlier.

"That's about your speed," the other singer had said and while snarky, it had been brutally truthful.

The song was much like the other two she'd recorded and did little to highlight her versatility or her talent at composition.

But she'd been working on something different that was almost finished. She'd already worked on the melody and a good portion of the arrangement with the keyboard and computer tucked at the far side of the living room. The idea for the melody had stuck in her brain when she'd taken a basic triad of chords and inverted them, taking a tune that might have been melancholy and making it fun.

And who didn't like a fun kind of song like "Manic Monday" by the Bangles or Sheryl Crow's "All I Wanna Do"?

She finished making her coffee and since Robbie had already jumped on his computer, she did the same, slipping on headphones so she could replay the composition she'd already written. As she worked, she found herself bopping along to the beat and refining the words for the tune.

Lily had taken a spot at her feet and whenever she shifted on her chair, Lily's head would perk up, as if to check if Selene was okay. Selene would rub her head, and the dog would settle down again.

Every now and then, Selene would glance back over her

shoulder at Robbie, whose sole attention seemed to be on his laptop, brow furrowed as he worked.

But she was smiling as she ran through the composition a few more times and then prepared a file to send to Jason.

He'd probably think she was silly for changing up what they'd agreed to earlier, but her gut was telling her that this was the song that might make all the difference.

And if the Miami producer wanted to sign her, maybe Robbie and she could continue to explore what they were feeling for each other when he returned to his family and job with South Beach Security.

Armed with that thought, she smiled and sent the file to Jason. She hoped he'd check first thing in the morning and tweak what she'd done so they could make the final changes at the recording studio.

"Penny for your thoughts," Robbie said, making her jump in her seat and earning a sharp bark from Lily as she surged to her feet, ready to defend.

"YOU SCARED ME," Selene said and laid a hand over her heart as if to still its nervous beating. She also reached down to pet Lily and reassured her nothing was wrong.

"I'm sorry. I just couldn't resist seeing what it was that had you humming and smiling so happily," he said and peered past her at the dual computer monitors displaying what looked like music notation software and an audio mixer program.

"Is that how you compose?" he asked with a flip of his hand in the direction of the keyboard and screens.

"Depends. Sometimes I just play around on the guitar, but this one seemed better suited to the keyboard."

"It's more upbeat," he said, not that he was any judge of good music. He only listened to music while he was jogging and mainly for the beat to pace him.

"It is. I decided to do a different song tomorrow," she said and then looked away, as if afraid he'd see too much.

But he'd already seen what she was trying to hide. Gently cupping her chin, he urged her to face him. "Rachel?" he asked with an arch of a brow.

She hunched her shoulders up and down and did a little head bob. "She might have had a point."

Robbie considered that and said, "What's her story anyway?"

Another shrug warned him that Selene was uncomfortable, but he pressed her. "I'll find out anyway when I do an internet search."

The hesitation came again as Selene worried her lower lip in that familiar gesture before she blurted out, "I understand her. She made the same mistake I did in falling for the wrong man. He didn't abuse her, but he knocked her up and then dumped her when his career took off."

"They were in a band together?" he asked and urged her from the chair to walk with him to the couch. With a hand command, he urged Lily to follow, and she did, pleasing him with how she understood the simple command.

They sat on the couch, Lily at their feet, and Selene snuggled into his side while she completed the story. "They were the lead singers. If you ask me, she's what made him look and sound good."

"Where is he now?" Robbie asked as he stroked his hand up and down her arm in a soothing caress.

"Dead. OD'd on a mix of alcohol and half-a-dozen drugs. The only good thing he did was leave a life insurance settlement that made Rachel and her daughter a little more secure. But she still has to work a day job while chasing her dreams at night."

"I give her credit for doing that. It must not be easy," Robbie said, appreciating what it took for people to follow their dreams. His Cuban family had done the same after escaping Castro's regime. It had taken years of hard work and dedication before his grandfather had been able to open South Beach Security and even more labor and sacrifice to make it what it is today.

"It isn't easy and that's why I cut her some slack," Selene admitted and swiveled slightly to peer up at him, eyes narrowed. "You don't think she has something to do with the notes, do you?"

He locked his gaze on hers and cupped her cheek. "It's too early to tell. We're still waiting for any results from the CBI's CSI unit, and Sophie and I have only just started working our way through a list of suspects."

Her eyes widened in confusion. "How many do you have?"

"Pretty much anyone you have contact with at the bar and recording studio. Bart as well," he admitted with a nonchalant shrug.

"So many people," she said in a tiny voice and her body trembled against his side.

He got it. *So many people who could want to hurt her.*

Stroking his thumb across her cheek, he said, "You have lots of people to protect you and who love you."

Her eyes shimmered with unshed tears, but a shadow of a smile drifted across her lips. She reached up and raked her fingers through his hair, then trailed her hand down tenderly across his bruised cheek. Wincing slightly, she said, "Does it still hurt?"

"Only when I smile," he said, then grinned and faked a grimace.

She chuckled and shook her head, but then her almost electric blue gaze darkened. She rose slightly on her knees, until she was eye to eye, lip to lip, with him.

"Selene?" he asked, wanting to be sure of what she wanted.

She answered by leaning in and skimming a kiss across his

lips, the touch a hesitant exploration as she returned to kiss him over and over.

He cradled her back, offering comfort and support as the kiss deepened.

Her breath soughed against his lips as she broke away for a second, but then returned, opening her mouth to his. Pressing her body to his, he drew her in tighter until they were breast to chest and his body responded, hardening against her softness.

She shivered then and he tempered his hold, loosening it so she could draw back and meet his gaze.

She licked her lips, then bit her lower one and shook her head, as if in denial of what she was feeling.

"I'm not… It's been…" She shook her head harder then and looked away before blurting out, "I'm not sure of what I want. I'm sorry."

He clasped her cheek and tenderly urged her to meet his gaze. "I'm a patient man, Selene. I would never rush you or hurt you."

Through incipient tears, she nodded. "I know," she said, voice hoarse, and in a softer tone added, "I do. I do."

It was almost as if she was trying to convince herself. To truly believe he wouldn't damage her as other men had, which made his heart hurt at the pain she'd suffered.

"Whenever you're ready, Selene," he said and meant it, even if whenever turned out to be never.

She nodded but pushed away from him and he loosened his hold, letting her slide off his lap and back onto the sofa cushions.

A phone rang from somewhere in the direction of the dining table with a ringtone he didn't recognize.

But Selene did.

She bolted from the sofa, raced to the table and answered as Lily started barking, sensing some kind of upset.

Her soft, anguished "No" tore through him as did the pain in her gaze.

He laid his hand at her waist to steady her as she swayed but then stiffened her back. "We'll be there soon," she said and hung up.

"What's wrong?" he asked, worried that something had happened to either her pregnant sister Rhea or his police chief cousin Jackson.

"Someone set fire to the recording studio building."

Chapter Ten

Selene fought the quaking in her body as the firefighters squelched the last of the flames at the corner of the building housing the studio. She tightened her hold on Lily's leash to keep the pittie at her side.

Above the smoking pile of rubbish, broken branches and twigs that had been set ablaze, *Selene* was written in streaky black paint, marring the colorful mural.

A firefighter hosed water up and down the area and as the water touched the black paint, it trickled down the side of the building like mascara running down after a bout of tears.

Robbie laid a hand on her shoulder and squeezed. "It's not that bad. See," he said as the firefighter turned the hose upward and her name disappeared from the wall, the black paint melding with the grime from the small fire.

"It's not that bad but the building owner is furious," Jason said as he approached and gestured to a man standing off to one side. The building owner, Robbie guessed.

"It won't happen again. We'll get in some CCTV cameras and start monitoring the area if that's okay with the building owner," Robbie said to reassure him.

Jason brushed his fingers through his hair, his gaze apologetic as he turned it on Selene. "It can't happen again because if it does, he's going to toss my recording studio out of the building. I can't afford for that to happen."

His gaze drifted down to where Lily sat at her feet and a sour look erupted on his face. "Is that yours?"

"*She* is Selene's. Her name is Lily, and we rescued her from the shelter," Robbie said. Beneath his hand, Selene's body shook but then her shoulders pulled back and she straightened her body as strength flooded through her.

"That's right. Lily is my dog. More importantly, if Robbie says something like this won't happen again, it won't," she said, certainty in her voice.

Jason glanced back and forth between them, doubtful, but then dipped his head in the direction of the older man, who was now standing by the fire chief at his truck. "I'll speak to the owner about that and the cameras."

"Good. So I guess we'll see you later for the recording session," Robbie pressed, wanting there to be no doubt it was business as usual.

Jason's gaze skipped from him to Selene and his mood softened a little at the mention of the recording session. With a reluctant nod, he said, "But a little later. I haven't been up this late for a gig in a long time."

Robbie risked a glance at his smartwatch as Selene confirmed the time on her phone. 2:00 a.m. Later than he'd realized since he'd lost track of time while working and then spending time with Selene.

"Let's say one. That'll give me time to get some rest and work on that new material you sent me," Jason said.

Selene clasped her hands in front of her and dipped her head in thanks. "I really appreciate that, Jason."

"You know I'd do anything for you, Selene," he said and flipped his hand toward the fire truck. "Let me speak to the owner."

"I'll go with," Robbie said and squeezed her shoulder again. "Will you be okay here?"

SELENE NODDED AND wrapped her arms around herself. "I will. I've got Lily with me."

He skimmed his hand down her back and then walked away with Jason to speak to the building owner and fire chief.

She stood there, gaze fixed on the pile of smoking garbage and wood and dirty water that streamed down the sidewalk and onto the street, carrying away the grime. Maybe taking Jason's recording studio with it if they couldn't stop what her stalker was doing.

She couldn't let that happen any more than she could let the stalker ruin this chance of a lifetime for her.

Or let Robbie be the only person responsible for saving that dream.

After her husband's abuse and her harrowing experience during her kidnapping, she'd gone to a therapist who'd helped her through the trauma and also helped her regain some control over her life.

At times she'd felt that control slipping, especially after she'd started receiving the notes.

But no longer.

Lily barked up at her as if sensing her upset, and Selene bent and rubbed the dog's head, earning some doggy love that provided the last bit of courage she needed to walk over and join the men who were speaking to the owner.

The older man eyed her as she neared and held out her hand. "Selene Reilly. I want to offer my apologies for what's happened at your building."

After a surprised, wide-eyed gaze, the man grasped her hand and pumped it enthusiastically, his earlier anger apparently abated. "Mike Baxter. It's nice to meet you. I've been to the bar to hear you sing several times."

"Thank you. I appreciate that and if you'd like, I can arrange for a nice meal for you at one of the shows," she said, grateful that he was a fan and hoping to make up for the damage and inconvenience caused by the small fire.

Baxter smiled. "My wife and I would love that," he said and then looked at the two men with a little less adoration than he'd provided Selene. "And hopefully these two can keep their promises about protecting my property."

"I trust Robbie and if he says he can do it, he will," she said, hoping that her words would offer the final reassurance to quell the owner's worries.

Baxter grunted and groused, "He better." Without a further word, he ambled away to an expensive sedan parked across the street.

Jason scratched his head and with a laugh said, "Your charm soothed the savage beast."

She playfully nudged his shoulder with hers. "Let's hope my music does the same for the producer."

Jason grinned and said, "No doubt it will. Which means I should get going so we can finish it later."

She hugged him and he strolled down the block to a well-used army-green Jeep Wrangler. The lights flashed on and off as he unlocked it, entered and then drove away, waving at them as he passed by.

"We should get going as well," Selene said, but Robbie hesitated, his attention focused on the remnants of the fire as the firemen spread the remaining bits of trash and wood and wet it down.

"What's the matter?" she asked, noticing his interest.

"He didn't want to burn down the building, just get our attention, but it is an escalation. Again," he said and brushed his fingers across his cheek.

She mimicked his action, grimacing at the bruise and his black eye, which was now a mix of purples and yellows as he healed. She was tempted to say "I'm sorry" again but held back the apology.

Instead, she twined her fingers with his, and in a determined voice, she said, "We will find him and stop him."

Because it was a *we*. They were a team now and, she hoped in the future, maybe more.

ROBBIE LAY IN bed as he slowly woke, his mind replaying all that had happened in the last few hours.

Replaying Selene's words that together they would find and stop her stalker.

He didn't doubt that they would, but the escalation with the physical attack and fire worried him. A lot.

It was probably too soon for CBI's CSI unit to have DNA info or even the fingerprints. He worried that because of the expensive and slightly uneven cotton paper of the envelopes and notes it would be difficult to get good photos or scans of any prints.

Not to mention that there might be many different prints since several people could have handled the items. Except for the note left last night.

It angered him that someone had been able to leave it without anyone noticing it. Including him.

Before they'd gotten the call about the fire, he'd hopped on the bar's server to view the camera feeds, but they hadn't been much help. No one had gone into the greenroom while Selene had been performing. Just Selene and her bandmates had entered and then there had been the bedlam as the new group had arrived.

Yet more people to add to the list of possible suspects. Way too many.

That pushed him from bed earlier than normal. As he entered the main living area, the sun was barely a sliver on the horizon as dawn approached.

He'd barely gotten a few hours of restless sleep.

His first priority: coffee. He'd need the jolt of caffeine and sugar to both get and keep him going.

He found Lily lying by Selene's door. The pittie popped her head up when she heard him and then followed him to the kitchen.

Priorities shifted and he fed Lily and after, took her for a quick walk so she could relieve herself. He hated leaving Selene alone in the condo, so he kept close to the door of the building.

Lily did her duty quickly and they returned to the condo, where Lily tagged after him as he went to the kitchen to finally make his coffee.

In just minutes the coffee was dripping into the carafe and he heated some milk since he liked adding so much that his coffee got too cold too quickly. He made himself a large mug that he took over to the dining table where his laptop sat, waiting for him.

As she had before, Lily followed him and then settled at his feet with a contented sigh.

Yet another priority was to let Sophie and Ryder know about the new note and last night's fire. He'd have to get them the evidence for analysis and hopefully, Ryder could get the fire marshal's report, which might provide some useful info.

Opening his e-mail program, he jotted off his report to them and then searched the internet for information on Selene's bandmates as well as the group that had performed after them.

Like Sophie, he preferred to look at some things offscreen, so he took down their names on a pad next to his laptop. Wrote down some other things that drew his attention.

When he got to the second group, his radar started pinging. It had been a basic rock group. Drummer, bassist, guitarist and singer. It made his radar ping even louder because he could have sworn he'd seen five people enter the greenroom during that chaotic shift of performers.

Pulling up the video he'd downloaded from the bar's servers, he fast-forwarded to those moments, and a solid beep, like a missile locking in on its target, confirmed what he'd remembered.

Five bodies went into the greenroom when the new band—Dodger Dogs—had arrived.

Hopping back on the internet, he pulled up the Dodger Dogs website and went to the page with info on the band members. All four of them.

Flipping between that page and the videos, he identified the four men and the one who wasn't part of the group. Unfortunately, the fifth man managed to hide well, keeping his head down where the shadow of his baseball cap hid his features, and the turned-up collar of his denim jacket obscured his lower face.

Robbie sped the video past the point where Selene, her bandmates and he had left to go to dinner.

Scott came into view twice, warning the band of the countdown to their performance.

A flurry of activity followed Scott's second warning as the group exited. All five of them and once again, the unknown fifth person kept his identity hidden. At one point, the Dodger Dogs' drummer had looked back at him as if wondering who he was, but then the band went into the wings and out of sight of CCTV cameras.

Switching to views of the stage and bar, Robbie searched for any sign of that fifth man, but he wasn't in either location. But he detected activity along stage left much like he had during Selene's first set.

But it was too dark and the video too grainy to see who was there.

Robbie muttered a curse and quickly sped through the video feeds for the main corridor and back door, but his unknown suspect never appeared again.

Impossible, he thought. *How had he gotten in and out?*

Flipping back to the point where the second band had come in, he realized the fifth man had joined them from the small hall that led to stage left. A hall without any kind of CCTV, a problem he intended to have corrected when he also kept his promise to the owner of the recording studio building.

Blowing out a heavy sigh, he thought, *So much to do.*

ROBBIE WAS SO focused on his work that he hadn't even noticed she had come into the room and made herself a cup of coffee. But Lily had as the dog hurried to Selene's side for the head rubs she seemed to love.

But as she neared the table, Robbie raised his mug without ever looking her way and said, "Would you please refresh this?"

"You are something," she said with a chuckle.

"Sophie says the same thing," he said as she approached. But when she got close, he rose and gently cradled her waist with his hand.

"Thank you in advance," he said and skimmed a kiss across her lips before returning to his work.

I could get used to mornings like this. She made him a fresh mug, brought it over and sat next to him, Lily tucked close to her feet.

"You were very intense a moment ago," she said and brushed her hand through the tousled waves of his hair. It looked like he had repeatedly jammed his fingers through it, possibly in frustration.

He tipped the chair back on two legs and put his hands behind his head in a way that made his leanly muscled chest seem even more muscled. With another gusted sigh, he said, "What do you know about the bar's history?"

She looked upward as she tried to dig up what the bar's owner had told her about the location. Facing him once again, she shrugged and said, "It's old. I think it was built in the 1880s when 16th Street became popular."

"And it's probably been renovated a few times by now."

"Within landmark rules," she added.

"Maybe a good thing. I'll have to pull up building plans so I can see if there are hidden holes or other openings we haven't covered with cameras," he said and dropped the chair back onto all four legs.

"You saw something?" she asked, catching his worried vibes.

"I did," he said and attacked the keys quickly before flipping the laptop around to show her an image.

Clearly a man, she thought, taking in the image. A black hoodie just like the other night's assailant. Basic denim jacket. A baseball cap. She shifted closer to peer at it, thinking it looked familiar.

"Can you make it sharper so we can make out the logo?" she said, circling her index finger around that area of the baseball cap.

"I'll try," he said. He whipped the laptop back around and got to work, his look intense as his fingers flew across the keys.

Barely a few minutes had passed when he showed her a sharper image of that portion of the ball cap.

Unfortunately, while it was sharper, it wasn't enough for her to identify the logo. At least not yet.

"Can you print that out?" she asked.

He nodded and within a second, the whir of the printer said she'd soon have the copy she wanted.

His phone vibrated to warn of a text message, and he snapped it up to read it.

"Soph and Ryder will be here in ten minutes with breakfast. Ryder is going to take the note to the bureau's CSI staff. Sophie is going to join us to help secure the condo and recording studio buildings. Maybe some more cameras at the bar. We'll talk about what else to do while we eat," he said, and his stomach grumbled as if to emphasize the *eat* part of his statement.

"You are a bottomless pit," she said and rose, intending to set the table for their guests.

"Sophie says the same thing all the time," Robbie said and put aside his laptop to rise and help her as she set out plates and cutlery.

They had just finished doing that and making a fresh pot of coffee when Sophie and Ryder buzzed to announce their arrival.

Lily barked at the sound of the intercom and rushed to the door, recognizing they were going to have visitors.

"Good girl," she said, rewarding her, especially as the dog barked at Sophie and Ryder as they entered. "They're friends. Sit," she said, and Lily obeyed and let the couple pass and walk to the table to join Robbie.

As the trio sat around the table to discuss developments and what to do, Selene sat back and listened, trying to understand what they were planning. Her mind whirled with how much there was to do in such a short time. Occasionally she would reach down and pet Lily, reinforcing their connection.

It didn't surprise her when they video-called their cousin Trey in Miami to have South Beach Security help them out.

ROBBIE HATED TO put any more on Trey, who not only had the burden of assuming leadership of SBS, but was also dealing with a newborn at home with his detective wife Roni.

"It's not a problem, *primo*," he said and his cousin Mia, who was expecting her first with her tech billionaire husband, echoed the statement.

"Whatever you need, we're here and you know John can run things through his program as well," Mia said.

John Wilson, Mia's husband, had created a predictive program that could identify possible outcomes. SBS had used the program for several investigations and a beta version of the program was in use by various police departments.

"That would be a huge help. I've got a big list of suspects, and I need to weed out who might not be a likely stalker. Plus, I'd like any background info on them."

"Just send the list over," Mia said with a wave of her hand.

"Will do," Robbie confirmed.

Sophie quickly added, "We need to get some cameras installed. Ryder provided the names of suppliers and some installers—can you arrange to monitor them?"

"I can. Just get us the links to access their feeds," Trey said with a nod and a relaxed smile, but Robbie noticed the dark smudges beneath his eyes that hinted at nights interrupted by a newborn's needs.

"I appreciate it. Get some rest. Roni too," he said and ended the video feed.

Robbie peered at everyone around the table. "Seems like we all have our jobs to do."

Ryder picked up last night's note that had been transferred into a plastic bag. "I'll get this analyzed and see where we stand on the earlier evidence."

"If you lay out your ideas for the cameras, I'll coordinate with the installers and Trey," Sophie said.

"Great," he said and glanced at Selene. "You have your recording session but after that, I'd love to go back to the bar and look around."

Selene dipped her head in agreement. "I'm good with that."

Robbie tapped the table with flat hands. "We have a plan. Let's hope we can catch this guy soon."

He rose, a signal to the others to get going as well. But as he walked Sophie and Ryder to the door, his sister looked at

Selene, leaned close to him and whispered, "Don't lose perspective."

"I won't," he said, even though his feelings for Selene were already impacting the investigation. Not that he didn't give each and every case his all, but this one was different.

This one was about something more than just getting justice.

It was about the future. A future that hadn't included a significant other and family only a few short weeks ago.

But now there was Selene and maybe she was all he'd ever needed.

Chapter Eleven

Selene listened through the headphones to the arrangement she had sent Jason the night before.

Even with the upset and loss of time from last night's fire, Jason had managed to beef up the arrangement by adding several instruments digitally. The brightness of the beat had been amped higher with a jingly-jangly tambourine and snappy drum accompaniment. Horns and violins added depth during what would be the chorus of the song.

"This is amazing, Jason. You did a wonderful job," she said and gave him a thumbs-up and a big smile.

From inside the recording booth, Jason mimicked her action with a tired grin. "I love the tune. I think you were right to change it."

"Thank you. I'm ready when you are," she said and with another thumbs-up, the melody played in her headphones.

She waited for the right moment and then sang and as she did so, she found herself tapping her feet and bouncing along to the catchy tune. The song was infectious, rousing joy she hadn't felt in a long time. Because of that, the song had depth she hadn't expected for a tune that was supposed to be all about fun.

As she finished, her heart swelling with that joy, she glanced into the recording studio where both Robbie and Jason were on their feet, clapping.

Jason leaned forward to hit a button and his voice erupted across her headphones. "Wow, Selene. I love it."

"I do too, but do you think we could add some harmony during the chorus? Me in a major third and then a fifth?" she said. She picked up her guitar and played the chord, vocalizing part of the harmony to confirm.

"I like it, but how about—toward the end—changing it to a minor third and fifth for a little variation?" Jason suggested.

"I'm game," she said and waited for the music to start up. As the chorus started, she sang along in that higher key, creating the first bit of the harmony. When it came to the last chorus, she tried to do the minor chord, but it didn't feel right to her.

Shaking her head, she said, "I don't know about that."

"I agree. Let's stick to the major chord. Pick it up just before and we'll record it again," Jason said and a beat later, the melody played, and she recorded the final chorus.

"I think that's a wrap," Jason said and did another thumbs-up.

She hated to press, but this was so important to her. "Can I just hear it one last time before you work on adding that other harmony?"

Nodding, Jason said, "Of course."

Selene sat in the recording booth, feeling on edge as she listened to her creation. To the song that she thought might push her over the edge and get her signed with a major producer.

When the song finished, that joy filled her again along with a sense of accomplishment.

"Thank you, Jason," she said, slipped off the stool, and walked out of the booth to meet Jason and Robbie, who were waiting for her just outside the recording area.

She rushed into Jason's arms and hugged him, overjoyed by what they had just done.

She approached Robbie a little more slowly but as he wrapped his arms around her and rocked her, it was like a homecoming.

He brushed a kiss across her temple and whispered, "You are amazing. So beautiful and talented. That song… It's a hit."

"Thank you," she said and inched up on tiptoe to kiss him.

ROBBIE TIGHTENED HIS hold around her waist and deepened the kiss, overcome by the emotions that had spilled from her and into him.

But at a strangled cough from Jason, he tempered the kiss and let Selene drift back down onto her feet.

"We should go. Sophie texted me that she's downstairs and I'd like to see how that's going," he said and turned to walk away, but not before catching the look Jason shot him and then Selene.

There was definitely more there than just business when it came to Selene. But there was something else there that sent a little chill through him.

That meant Jason was going to stay on the suspect list for a little longer until Robbie and the team could confirm that his feelings for Selene hadn't gotten twisted and become violent.

"I'll send you the final mix by tomorrow so you can fire it off to the producer," Jason said with a wave good-bye.

"Thank you again, Jason," Selene called out, her voice musical as she did so.

"Later, Jason," Robbie added and did a little salute to bid the other man good-bye.

"Later," Jason said neutrally, but Robbie didn't miss the slight inflection that said *much later* as in *never*.

When they reached the ground floor, Sophie was there with an installer who was up on a ladder by the front door.

Robbie hugged his sister and stepped onto the sidewalk to inspect what was happening.

One camera was already up on the far corner of the building. It would catch anyone coming by on the sidewalk as well as most of the front of the building, including where the fire had been set the night before.

That area was already clean of the remnants of the fire and only a slight smoke stain remained on the mural. A touch-up with paint would remove the last traces of the incident.

Glancing back toward the front door, he took in the two women in his life.

His sister Sophie was as no-nonsense as could be. She wore faded jeans, a cropped T-shirt that hugged her lean body and a blue blazer that dressed up the entire look.

Selene was ethereal with her flowing boho chic skirt in a kaleidoscope of earth tones. A loose rust-colored blouse couldn't hide her generous curves, and his body tightened with need at the memory of her pressed against him.

Sensing his perusal, she smiled and waved a hand. Her many bracelets danced on her wrist and sunlight gleamed off the rings on her long, elegant fingers.

He pictured those fingers moving on him the way they loved the strings of her guitar and muttered a curse.

Get a grip, Robbie. You've got a job to do, he reminded himself and walked back to the front door.

"It looks good," he said and hugged his sister again, grateful she was still there with him and not in Miami.

Miami. At some point the two of them might be returning. Or maybe just him if Sophie decided to stay with Ryder.

As he released his sister, she eyeballed him. "Everything okay?"

"It is. Since you've got everything under control here, I was going to head to the bar to plan out those extra cameras and check out how someone could have snuck in," he advised.

Sophie held up a perfectly manicured index finger in a bright red. "I was thinking about that last night, and I found some old blueprints for the building."

His sister and he had that weird twin connection even

though they weren't twins. She'd known exactly what he'd planned to do next. He would have gotten to it sooner but the fire had interfered.

"Gracias. Can you e-mail—"

"Already done, hermanito," she said, teasing her older brother.

Grinning, he hugged her hard and then grabbed hold of Selene's hand.

"Let's go to the bar and then back to the condo to walk Lily."

THE BAR'S OWNER wasn't available, but Ralph was just coming on duty and had no issue with letting them in, especially since the owner had approved Robbie adding some extra cameras to areas that were currently blind.

This meant that Robbie's first stop was the security office to check out the video feeds and areas they covered.

Selene hung back in the hall, watching him review the monitors and take notes on a pad he whipped from the pocket of the dark blue puffer vest they'd bought on the walk over because he'd been feeling Denver's late spring cold.

He'd slipped it on over his denim jacket which already covered a tan and blue flannel shirt and blue T-shirt. The blues in the fabrics just made his ocean-colored eyes even bluer while the tans highlighted the chocolaty brown of his wavy hair.

The faded jeans hugged his muscled legs and very nice butt.

As Robbie straightened from viewing the cameras, he offered her a puzzled look, as if wondering what she was thinking.

Not that she was going to share how she loved the look of him.

"How are they?" she said and pointed a finger in the direction of the monitors.

"Mostly good except for that back hallway and stage left.

Pretty much what I expected," Robbie said and whipped his phone out of his pocket. He flipped it open, turning it into almost a minitablet.

"Wow," she murmured in approval.

With a shrug, he said, "It helps when you almost live on your tech."

His thumbs sped across the screen and a second later, what looked like a very old blueprint popped up.

Using two fingers, Robbie zoomed in to display the worrisome areas of the hall and stage.

"Let's check this out," he said. Hand in hand, they walked down to the narrow hall that led to stage left.

When they reached the darker area by the wings, a chill erupted across her body, almost as if a ghost had walked through her. If you believed in that kind of thing, which she wasn't sure she did. Although she had experienced something like that when she'd done a private party at the historic Brown Palace Hotel that was rumored to have several resident spirits.

As Robbie went to walk deeper into the wings, she snagged his hand and pulled him back.

He gave her that puzzled look again, dark brown brows furrowed over that fathomless blue gaze.

"What's wrong?" he asked.

She hunched her shoulders and shivered. "I don't know. I've got a bad feeling about this."

Robbie peered back at the wings by stage left and then his gaze locked with hers. Cupping her cheek, he said, "I just have to check on something. There's no need to worry."

Reluctantly, she nodded and followed him, keeping tight to his back, a hand on his shoulder.

She didn't normally enter from stage left because of the location of the greenroom and after seeing a troublesome presence there last night, she worried about what they might find.

But there was nothing, and as they moved away from the curtains, a dim light illuminated the area by the wall.

Robbie paused, held up this phone and examined the blueprint. When he finished, he looked down as if searching the floor for something.

She tracked his gaze and almost at the same time, they noticed the line bisecting the long pine panels of the floor and a nearby recessed ring. Age had darkened the patina of the metal ring to the point that it blended with the color of the pine floor planks, especially given the dim lighting in the area.

Robbie closed his flip phone and tucked it into his jacket pocket. Reaching into his denim jacket, he pulled out a pocketknife, opened it, and pried the ring up so he could grab it.

As he did so that chill chased across her body again and she rubbed her hands up and down her arms, trying to drive it away.

Robbie noticed her motion. "Are you okay?"

"This is creeping me out," she admitted, worried about what might be beneath the stage.

"The blueprints show an open space beneath the stage and then a cellar and stairs to an area right by the kitchen. That's if it hasn't been closed up after over a hundred years," he explained and jerked the trapdoor open.

The door didn't creak as he opened it, despite the aged metal hinges. A slightly musty smell and cold air swept up through the opening which was about the size of an average person.

Robbie knelt, inspected the hinges and swiped his fingers across them. Rubbing his fingers together, he raised them so she could see the oily sheen on them.

"Someone's greased them so they wouldn't squeak and warn that they were using this trapdoor," he said and pulled a bandana from his pocket to wipe his fingers clean.

When he took a step toward the opening, she grabbed his hand again and jerked him back, more forcefully this time.

He faced her and said, "Don't worry. I'll be okay."

"Please don't go. I've got a bad feeling about this," she said and tightened her hold on his hand.

Grasping her hand in both of his, he said, "Mi amor. I have to do this to keep you safe. If someone was here last night and left you that note, they may have come through this door."

She couldn't argue with him but that didn't make her feel any better about what he was going to do. But she wasn't going to let him go alone.

"I'm coming with you," she said and inched her chin up defiantly, daring him to refuse.

Chapter Twelve

Robbie recognized that determined tilt of her head. He'd seen it more than once on his sister Sophie.

Because of that, he didn't argue. But he wiggled a finger in her face and said, "I go first."

She blew out a shaky breath and nodded. "You go first," she echoed.

He whipped out his phone, turned on the flashlight and directed it at the stairs.

He took the first step down and then another and another and as he did so, it felt like he was traveling into another century.

The floor beneath his feet was cobblestones with sandy soil compacted between them.

The foundation of the building was made of similar stones cemented together. Here and there were minor cracks where water stains streaked down to the floor. That explained the musty smell. Luckily, the foundation was mostly intact in this area of the basement.

Sweeping his phone flashlight across the area, he didn't see any other openings. He did the same to the floor, but the cobblestones made it hard to see any footprints. Though he thought he detected where some of the sand grout had been displaced.

If he followed what he thought was a trail, it led deeper into the cellar and into the area beneath the stage—possibly to the stairs and exit identified on the blueprint.

A footfall behind him alerted him to Selene coming down the stairs. As she did so, the dim stage light fell on her pale face and blue gaze dark with worry.

She joined him on the floor, and he gestured with his phone toward the other part of the cellar that had clearly been unused for some time.

Immense, ghostly cobwebs glinted in the corners of the space as he flashed his phone light at them.

"I think I see some disturbances in the sand," he said and highlighted them with the flashlight.

A second later, Selene snapped on her flashlight to add it to his, making the displacement of the sand a little more obvious.

"That way," he said and, hand in hand, they crept forward, staying on the trail they had exposed with the supports for the bar's stage to their left.

A creaking sound ahead warned them to pause.

A mistake, he realized as a louder snap and groan reverberated through the cellar.

Barely a breath later, the timbers holding up the stage shuddered and then began to buckle.

"Watch out," he screamed. He wrapped Selene in his arms and hauled her away from the dirt, dust and deadly beams and planks raining down on them.

The wood and debris pummeled his body, but all he thought was *Keep her safe.*

Until a two-by-four hit his head and dark circles danced around in his vision as silence filled the air after the stage's collapse.

SELENE COUGHED AS years of dirt and dust filled the air, scratching her throat.

Robbie's weight blanketed her above. The cobblestones and sand were rough, gritty and cold beneath her cheek.

Robbie moaned, slipped off her back and sat up.

As she came to her knees, it was impossible to miss the blood leaking down his face and the side of his head. His gaze was slightly dazed for a moment until it locked on her.

"Are you okay?" he asked and cupped her cheek with a dirt-streaked hand.

"I am but you're not. We need to get you to the hospital."

Light streamed into the cellar from where half the stage had collapsed. Suddenly Ralph was there, peering down, and as he saw them, he said, "Are you two okay?"

"We're okay," Robbie called up and shakily got to his feet.

He held his hand out to her and helped her stand. She tucked her hand into his and as he led her back to the trapdoor, which had been unscathed by the collapse, she noted the slashes and cuts in the puffer jacket he had just purchased. Every piece of damage to the jacket warned that Robbie had been injured by the debris that had pummeled them.

Or rather, him.

He'd borne the brunt of the collapse to protect her.

Once they were back on the main floor level, she tugged on his hand, forcing him to face her. When he did, confusion on his features, she stepped into his arms and hugged him. The slight tension and moan that escaped him warned that he was hurting.

"You saved me," she said and kissed his cheek.

ROBBIE DIDN'T KNOW what to say other than, "Anytime."

She jerked back, shook her head and slashed the air with her hand. "No, not anytime. This has gotten way too dangerous."

He waved his hands in the air to stop her. "We don't know that this has anything to do with our investigation."

Her dark brow sailed upward like a crow taking flight. "Really? The stage has been here like, what? A hundred or more years and now it collapses?"

He couldn't argue with her, but it was too late to put the brakes on this case.

"We don't have a choice. Your stalker is escalating, and we need to stop him."

Heavy footfalls sounded in the hallway at the rear of the wings and a second later, Ralph and Scott joined them by the trapdoor entrance.

Ralph peered at the trapdoor in surprise, as if unaware of its existence. Scott, however, didn't seem so surprised. His face had an almost blank stare as if he didn't understand.

"Lord, what happened?" Ralph asked and ran a hand through his salt-and-pepper hair. Before Robbie could answer, Ralph cursed and said, "The boss is going to flip when he sees the stage."

Robbie peered toward the area where about half the stage leaned down drunkenly before a yawning space close to stage right. No one would be performing there that night, but he suspected some repairs could make it usable quickly.

But first, they had to verify whether it was an accident or attempted murder.

"We'll get it fixed, but I need to call in our CBI contact—"

Ralph slashed his hands through the air. "No cops. Boss doesn't like cops on the premises."

"But he likes stalkers and murderers in the bar?" Selene said with an icy chill that shamed the other man into reluctant acceptance.

"Whatever. As soon as you make your call to CBI, you need to tell me what you're going to do about that," he said and gestured in the direction of the collapsed stage.

"Tell your boss we'll get it fixed," Robbie said.

Despite the collapse, he'd managed to hold on to his phone. But the protective screen was cracked and covered in dirt much like the rest of him and Selene. He shut off the flashlight and after, dialed his cousin Trey who immediately answered.

With his gaze locked on Selene's, he said, "Do you think you might find a general contractor in the area for us?"

AFTER RALPH'S ACQUIESCENCE, Robbie called in Ryder who brought his CSI team to examine the area as well as an EMT to check out Robbie's injuries.

Selene hovered nearby like a mother hen, listening to what the EMT had to say about the head wound and the assorted bruises all along Robbie's back and arms.

She winced at the sight of the half dozen or so purpling spots that had to be causing him pain. But if they were, he wasn't admitting to it.

The EMT had finished his exam and cleaned up the nasty scratch that ran from his eyebrow to just above his ear. Luckily it wasn't serious, although the EMT had expressed some concern that Robbie had a slight concussion.

Robbie shook his head to deny the EMT's assessment. "I didn't lose consciousness. I was just dazed for a second."

"That doesn't mean you didn't have a mild concussion," the EMT argued.

"I'm fine," Robbie said just as Sophie arrived on the scene, worry evident in features that were so much like Robbie's. Her aqua-blue eyes were dark with concern, her face pale as she swept her gaze over her brother.

"You look like—"

Robbie shot his hand up to stop her. "I'm fine. But I need you to get this place secured ASAP," he said, all business.

Sophie sucked in a deep breath, as if preparing to launch an objection, and then relented. "You are so stubborn," she said with a shake of her head and then enveloped her brother in a hug that had him groaning from the force of it.

"You deserve that," Sophie said, clearly both annoyed and worried for her brother.

Sophie faced her, stepped close and then hugged her while asking, "Are you okay?"

The comfort of the other woman's arms, so much like her sister Rhea's, nearly undid her. Tears came to her eyes and with her voice choked with emotion, she said, "As well as can be when someone might be trying to kill us."

And it was an *us* and not just a *me*. Twice now her stalker had hurt Robbie—and that pissed her off.

As she stepped away from Sophie, newfound anger and strength filled her core.

"We are going to find and stop this guy."

Ryder sauntered up to them and said, "We have to since he most definitely wanted you dead."

To prove that point, he held out his cell phone for all of them to look at a photo. "My CSI team found several support timbers that had been sawed and weakened. We also located a rope connected to one of the stage supports. We believe that once the rope was pulled, it took out the first timber and that caused a chain reaction."

"Like dominos tumbling down," Robbie said and went to drag his hand through his hair, but winced as he encountered his injury.

"Like dominos," Sophie echoed and glanced all around the bar area where they had gathered to await the result of the CSI team's investigation.

Selene mimicked Sophie's actions, tapping into what she was thinking.

"Whoever yanked that rope was here with us. May still be here," Selene said.

Ryder and Robbie shared a look before both of them glanced at Sophie. "Stay with Selene. We're going to find out who's here and who may have just left," Ryder said.

"Got it," Sophie confirmed and wrapped an arm around Selene's shoulders, offering support, but also comfort.

"I know it's upsetting," Sophie said and squeezed her upper arm.

Upsetting was the least of it. "Someone I know and trust just tried to kill us. I'm upset and more than that—I'm angry."

For too many years of her life, she'd let others control her and in a way, these actions were also about controlling her through fear.

"I want to take a walk around as well. Let them see me. Let them see that I'm not afraid," she said, pushing her shoulders back and straightening her spine.

Sophie peered at her, then nodded and smiled. "Let's go show them just who you are."

Raising her head a determined notch, they walked from the main bar area down the main hall that led to the greenroom, security office and then to the backstage entrance and narrow corridor to stage left.

In the security area, Robbie was working with the guard to review the camera feeds to see who had been around at the time of the incident.

A little farther down, in the greenroom, Ryder had corralled Ralph, Scott and members of the kitchen staff and was interrogating them as to their whereabouts and what they had seen.

Selene stood at that door, eyeballing the various workers. She wasn't all that familiar with the kitchen staff since they were back of house and she normally didn't interact with them. But she was familiar with Ralph and Scott.

It bothered her to think one of them might be responsible.

Ralph had been almost like a big brother when she'd first started working at the bar, making sure that she and her bandmates always had their table for meals and weren't bothered by any overenthusiastic patrons.

Scott was an enigma. Just a guy who called out the time and never really engaged with any of them or, for that matter, any others who worked at the bar. She'd tried multiple times to be friendly, but he'd been standoffish so she had given up.

As she met his gaze, he did a little twitch and looked away, obviously uncomfortable.

His discomfort grew even worse, and Ryder asked him for his personal info and any details about what he might have seen.

"I didn't see anything," Scott stammered and peered down at his shoes.

Ryder was about to press, but Ralph stepped in to stop the questioning.

"How about you let Scott get back to work and let me give you his info? I'll talk to him about what he might have seen," Ralph said, his tone conciliatory.

Ryder dipped his head in agreement. "You're free to go, Scott."

The younger man scurried away, shoulders hunched and head bowed, making him look like a whipped dog.

Ryder's keen gaze took that in but he pushed on, asking each of the kitchen workers what they'd been doing before and after the stage collapse.

As Selene listened, it seemed to her that there wasn't anything that might help them.

When the kitchen staff dispersed and went back to work, Ralph motioned them all deeper into the greenroom and closed the door behind them.

Leaning against the door, his look was almost weary as he said, "Scott is not your guy."

"What makes you say that?" Sophie asked.

"He's part of a special outreach program. He's very gentle and keeps to himself. That's why all he normally does with the performers is call out when they're due on stage," Ralph explained.

He faced Selene. "We don't tell people because we don't

want them to act differently around Scott. I hope you understand."

She did. It was why she didn't share the particulars of her background. When people found out about her abuse, it either made them uneasy or too nosy. Neither was good.

Even Robbie had acted differently around her at first, obviously aware of what she'd suffered.

"I understand, Ralph. You have my word—I won't say anything," she said and did a cross with her finger over her heart.

"We will keep that in mind," Ryder said, and Ralph provided him with Scott's info as well as a contact at the program that had placed Scott at the bar.

When Ryder finished jotting down the info, Ralph faced Selene once again, sadness in his gaze. "I'm sorry to say this, but the boss is furious about what's happened to the stage. He's not sure he wants you to perform here again until all your problems are taken care of."

Selene's knees went weak at his news but with her newfound strength, she handled it. "I understand and I will make good on having the stage fixed. Please let Mr. Smith know that we are going to find out who did this."

Sophie reached up and patted her shoulder. "We'll have someone by a little later to install those other cameras we discussed. Also, we've gotten a recommendation for a contractor in the area and as soon as the CBI's CSI team releases the crime scene, we'll get the repairs started."

"Thank you. I'll let the boss know," Ralph said, then he opened the door and hurried out.

Robbie came to the door, his look grim as he said, "CCTV caught someone exiting the building right after the collapse."

Chapter Thirteen

The CSI team released the scene, leaving Ryder, Selene and Robbie to return to the condo to regroup.

Sophie stayed behind to oversee the installation and connections to the new cameras and talk to a general contractor about the repairs.

Lily greeted them with barks and excited jumps as they entered the condo. Selene knelt to hug the dog and earned doggy kisses that had her smiling despite the severity of her situation.

"Let me take Lily for a quick walk," Robbie said, leashed the pittie, and rushed out of the condo.

"It was a good idea to get Lily. She'll be a good companion and guard dog for you," Ryder said as he watched Robbie leave with the pit bull mix.

"She will, I think. Can I get you anything? Coffee?" she asked the CBI agent.

"Coffee would be nice," he said and then walked over to the dining table to wait for Robbie.

Selene hurried to the kitchen to make some coffee for the men and a pot of tea for herself. Her Irish-born mother had poured a spot of tea and sat with her whenever she or her sister Rhea needed someone to listen.

That simple act of heating the water, measuring out the loose tea leaves and letting them steep in her mother's fine china teapot had always brought comfort.

Today was no different.

Or maybe it is, she thought as Robbie returned and something shifted inside her as his presence and Lily's caused even greater comfort.

She warmed milk for Robbie's coffee and asked Ryder how he wanted his as Lily rushed to her side after being unleashed.

"I can make my own," he said, and Robbie agreed. "Me too."

She waved them off. "I need something to do. So what will it be, Ryder? I already know Robbie likes it light and sweet."

"Black will do," Ryder said.

It didn't take long to make their coffees, fix her cup of tea and add some shortbread cookies—another ritual of her mother's—onto a tray that she took to the table.

As she set the tray down and sat, Lily at her feet, she realized that Robbie had called in the SBS team. Their worried faces filled the TV screen as Robbie finished his report.

"It looks like our suspect moved northward toward Union Station and Commons Park. He had to have passed several traffic cameras, webcams or ATM cameras. I know you're already searching for other feeds in the area south of the bar, but do you think you can track down these northward feeds?" Robbie said.

"I'll talk to John about adding them to our search," Mia confirmed.

"I wish I could do it, but my hands are full right now," Robbie said apologetically. She guessed that Sophie and he were normally the ones to work on those kinds of things, but clearly they were unavailable at the moment.

"It's not a problem. What else can we do?" Trey asked, his blue gaze intense and so much like Robbie's, she thought.

All the cousins had similar features, with strong Roman noses, intense light eyes, dark hair and dimpled chins. A good-looking family that suddenly had her picturing what a baby with Robbie might look like.

Dark-haired and blue-eyed since they both had that in common.

"Did Wilson's program give us any probabilities on our possible suspects?" Robbie asked, reminding Selene that they'd sent a long list of names to the SBS team the day before.

Mia nodded. "John sent over some preliminary predictions just a few minutes ago. I'll send it over as soon as the meeting's over."

"That's appreciated and gracias," Robbie said.

"Yes, thank you. I don't know how I could ever repay you for all that you're doing for me," Selene said, grateful she had their help and protection.

"You're family, and we help family. We'll get to work and send you what we have as soon as possible," Trey said and ended the call.

Ryder cradled his mug of coffee in his hands and swiveled in his chair to face them. "I guess we wait and see what my team can get from the two crime scenes and that last note. I doubt we'll glean much from the fire, but it might be better at the bar. I didn't see any gloves on our suspect from the CCTV feed so hopefully there's touch DNA on the rope at the scene."

"I've got video of someone from last night and now we have these images. I'm going to work with them to estimate height and weight. Combined with Wilson's predictions, we may be able to narrow our list of suspects," Robbie said and opened his e-mail program to display the message from Mia.

A shocked gasp escaped her at the list of the top three most probable suspects and at her feet, Lily rose and peered up at her, sensing her upset.

Bart and Jason were both at 75 percent. Ralph was at 65 percent.

"I don't believe it. Jason and Ralph would never do anything to hurt me," she said and walked away, pacing back and forth, careful to avoid tripping over Lily, who refused to leave her side.

As she paced, she considered why the two men who had been so nice and helpful to her would now be trying to harm her.

Robbie hurried to her side and laid a gentle hand on her shoulder to still the nervous motion. "It's just a probability and it could be wrong."

She nailed him with her gaze. "It's a program you think is highly accurate, isn't it?"

With a reluctant dip of his head, he admitted it. "We do. It's been right before."

Looking away, she sucked in a deep breath and then blew it out harshly. "I guess we'll have to see."

Ryder called out from the table. "You didn't mention Bart. Do you think he could harm you?"

Selene tilted her head from side to side, wondering if the determined waiter had bad intentions directed at her. With a lift of her shoulders, she said, "Honestly, I don't know him well enough to say. I've always thought he was just a waiter with a crush and who liked a good tip."

"We'll have to remedy that, then. And find out all we can about Ralph and Jason," Robbie said and then reached up to stroke her hair. As he did so, it seemed like a halo of dust surrounded her much like Pigpen in the Peanuts series.

"And maybe it's also time we got cleaned up."

Robbie nodded. "You go first and maybe we can think about dinner after I'm done showering."

"And I'm going to get Sophie. I think she'd probably like to have dinner with you and make sure you're okay," Ryder said and eyeballed Robbie to emphasize that he wasn't going to get out of sharing a meal with them.

"I think that sounds lovely," Selene said. And it also sounded normal at a time when normal didn't seem possible.

She brushed a kiss across Robbie's cheek and hurried from the room to take a much-needed shower to wipe away the grit from the stage collapse.

Lily followed her into her bedroom. When Selene closed the door, Lily took a spot at the entrance, watching as Selene quickly stripped off her dirt-stained clothes and tossed them into the hamper. She turned the shower water as hot as she could stand it and then stepped in and let the water wash over her for long minutes.

Grayish-brown dirt circled the drain much like it seemed her newfound musical career might be doing. Another incident at the recording studio building and she'd be done there. Same for the bar if they were even lucky enough to get the stage fixed quickly.

And what if the Miami music producer heard about all her problems? Would she want to sign her with these issues going on?

But Robbie had said they'd find her stalker and now, would-be murderer. And SBS had solved many cases and even helped to rescue her when she'd been kidnapped. She had to trust that they would put an end to this threat to her life and career.

Finishing her shower, she toweled off the strands of her shoulder-length hair and slipped into jeans and a T-shirt for their upcoming dinner.

Rushing out into the condo's living space with Lily at her side, she realized Robbie was back at work on his laptop.

He looked up as she entered and offered her a tired smile. "You look great, but how do you feel?"

"With my hands," she said with a laugh and mimicked lobster-like claws with her hands. "Sorry, it's an old joke for Rhea and me."

He shut his laptop, pushed to his feet and walked over. He

was about to cradle her cheek with his dirt-streaked hand but then pulled it back with a harsh laugh.

"Don't want to dirty you. I'd like to know more about you and Rhea. She is family now and so are you."

"We used to joke a lot as kids. My parents always made us laugh," she said, and his face grew unfocused as unshed tears filled her vision. Lily did a little whine and looked up at her, ever attentive to Selene's moods.

Robbie did touch her then, trailing his thumb across her cheek to wipe away a tear as Lily bumped her head against her calf, also offering comfort.

"It must be hard for you now that they're gone."

With a few quick, abrupt nods, she said, "It is. But I have Rhea and now Jax. Plus you and your family."

"Ryder too, I think. I see how Sophie looks at him. I think he's the one for her," Robbie said and with the way he was looking at her, she thought that maybe he thought *she* might be the one as well.

But could that feeling last past this investigation? Was it possible that Sophie and he would find happiness in Denver?

"I think she loves him and that Ryder loves her," she said just as a buzz erupted from the intercom. Lily's barks echoed through the condo, warning that the couple had arrived.

"I SHOULD GO SHOWER," Robbie said and rushed from the room, grateful for the arrival of Sophie and Ryder because the conversation with Selene was leading to a possibly difficult discussion.

He didn't doubt how he was feeling for her.

But he didn't know how she felt or if she was even ready for a relationship given all that she'd suffered in her past life and what was happening now.

Patience, he told himself, recalling the discussion he'd had just days earlier with his psychologist cousin Ricky. And while

Selene didn't want to be treated differently, he did have to handle her with kid gloves until she was ready for more.

She'd been ready for something as simple as holding hands and seemed to be getting used to not recoiling when he came close.

And because he wanted to be close to her again, he hurried through his shower. That and the fact that the strong rush of the water against his back stung against areas bruised by the debris from the collapse.

As he stepped out of the stall and caught sight of his back in the bathroom mirror, he winced at the many patches of mottled blue.

He had been lucky not to break any bones.

Gingerly toweling off his hair to avoid the ugly scratch along one side of his head, he rushed out to the bedroom, got dressed and then hurried to the living area where Sophie, Ryder and Selene were seated at the table.

Lily rushed over to greet him, excitedly jumping up at him until he quieted her with a few head rubs and a command to sit.

Sophie surged to her feet and came over to inspect him, motherly concern on her face, especially as her gaze traveled across the raw scratch at the side of his face. "Are you really feeling okay?"

With a quick lift of his shoulders, he said, "Sore, but okay. We were lucky."

"Yes, you were. We need to catch this guy before anything else happens," Sophie said. She came to his side, slipped her arm through his and walked him to the table.

"That's the plan," Robbie said flippantly.

"And the plan for dinner is to hit Alberto's. I'd like to meet Bart and get a feel for him before we run him through all the databases," Ryder said and then looked at Selene. "Any possibility I could meet Jason?"

Selene's lips tightened into a thin slash. "We're done recording. He's supposed to send my final files by tomorrow, but we normally do that exchange electronically."

"What was your read on him?" Ryder said and turned his attention to Robbie.

"Competent. Supportive of Selene. Jealous," he said, recalling the way the other man had looked at them. At the last second, he added, "Maybe even threatening. Something rubbed me the wrong way about him and Bart."

Sophie eyeballed him and then skipped her gaze to Selene. "Could it be because *you're* interested in Selene too?"

The heat of embarrassed color filled his face, and a similar blush crept up Selene's neck to her cheeks.

"Real smooth, Sophie," he chastised, but then again, his sister and he didn't play games with each other. Directness that some saw as brusque at times had always been the way they communicated.

"I am interested in Selene and hope the feeling's mutual. But it's not just because of that. My gut says something is off with both of them. Ralph not so much," he admitted.

Sophie and Ryder were silent for a moment before Sophie finally said, "I've always trusted your gut. We'll run them and find out more."

Robbie nodded and as his stomach did a familiar little rumble, he held up an index finger. "But first—dinner and Bart."

ALTHOUGH THE RESTAURANT had outdoor seating that would have let them bring Lily, that area wasn't part of Bart's section, so they left Lily at the condo.

Robbie had wished they could bring her to see how the dog reacted to Bart once again since they said that dogs were a good judge of character.

But so were Sophie and Ryder and he hoped they would get a good read on the waiter.

The hostess seated them in Bart's area and in no time

the man came over, but there was no missing the tension in his body as he took note of Robbie and Ryder, who had that cop- or military-like look about him with his close-cropped hair and body posture.

"It's good to see you again, Selene," he said with a slight hesitation as he handed menus to all of them.

As Bart passed him the paper menu, the sleeve of his crisp white shirt shifted upward, revealing an angry scratch along his wrist.

"That looks painful. How did you get hurt?" Robbie said and motioned to the cut with his finger.

Bart jerked the sleeve down, almost angrily. "It's nothing. Would you like to hear today's specials?" he asked, quickly changing the topic.

Robbie met Ryder's gaze across the table and it was obvious the CBI agent had also noticed.

"I'd love to hear the specials," Sophie said, turning on the charm in the hopes honey might catch that fly.

Bart rattled them off and some of the tension eased from his body. "The appetizer is a locally made burrata with a salad of locally grown and organic tomatoes. The entrée is a frutti di mare with shrimp, clams and calamari in a tomato broth over squid ink linguini."

"Thank you," Sophie said with a dazzling smile. "I'll have both of those."

"They do sound wonderful. Me too," Selene said, also with a bright smile that yanked a hesitant one from Bart.

But his lips thinned into a narrow line as he turned his attention to Ryder and Robbie.

"Chicken parm," Ryder said and Robbie echoed the order, preferring traditional to any of the nouvelle Italian dishes on the menu.

Bart snapped his notepad closed. "I'll get those orders placed and get some bread out to you shortly."

He scurried away, leaving the couples to discuss the waiter.

"I'd like to know how he got that cut. Looks a lot like this," Robbie said and pointed to the scratch he'd gotten during the stage collapse.

"I agree. He was evasive," Ryder said and peered at Sophie. "What did you think?"

A quick up and down of her shoulders was followed by, "I'm not sure. My radar isn't pinging."

"Mine is," Robbie immediately countered, which earned an arched brow and stare from his sister.

"Yes, I'm partial," he said, well aware of what his sister thought, and met Selene's gaze.

A flush of color stained her cheeks as she stammered, "I know Bart's interested. But I've told him no, and he seemed okay with that."

Using air quotes in emphasis, he said, "Seemed okay."

A busboy swept by a second later, depositing a heaping basket of focaccia bread in the center of the table before rushing away.

Barely a second later, Bart returned with a bottle of Chianti that he was about to open when Robbie said, "Thanks, but we didn't order any wine."

Bart fixed him with an almost hostile glare. "Compliments of Alberto. He's a big fan of Selene's."

"Thank you, Bart. Please let Alberto know it's much appreciated," Selene said with a gentle smile that instantly tempered the man's hostility.

"I shall," Bart said with a harrumph that seemed almost theatrical as he poured each of them a glass of wine.

After he walked away, Robbie leaned close and, in low tones so only they could hear, he said, "He's staying on my list for now."

"Mine too. Once we finish our meal, I'm going to ask him

for some pages from that notepad to get a handwriting sample to compare to the notes," Ryder said.

Selene tipped her gaze upward, as if searching for something, and then said, "I've seen his handwriting. It doesn't look like that on the notes."

Robbie laid a hand on hers as he said, "Whoever wrote those notes probably tried to alter their handwriting. But there are unique traits that may remain, and an expert can detect those traits."

Selene seemed hesitant and Ryder confirmed what he'd said. "Robbie is one hundred percent right. The author of the notes likely disguised their handwriting. Do you have anything that Jason wrote by any chance?"

Tipping her head from side to side, contemplating the request, she said, "My birthday was last month, and he sent me a funny card I kept. It's back at the condo."

"Great. We'll take those specimens to CBI's handwriting expert to see what they have to say," Ryder said with a bop of his head.

Selene was quiet for a long moment, but then blurted out, "What if it's neither of them?"

Chapter Fourteen

Selene didn't want to think that either Bart or Jason was behind the notes and attacks. For that matter, she didn't want to think that anyone could want to hurt her.

"It's hard to imagine that I've done something—"

"*You* haven't done anything," Robbie said with a reassuring squeeze of her hand.

Selene released a sharp breath. "That's what the therapist repeatedly told me. That what my ex did to me was on him. Same for the two mountain men who kidnapped me," she said and then quickly tacked on, "And what about them? Aren't they more likely suspects?"

The trio of investigators at the table shared a look and in a gentle tone, probably to quiet the rising anger and upset in hers, Sophie said, "Ryder and I spoke to your ex, and he was cooperative. He had a solid alibi for the night Robbie was attacked and for last night's fire. We suspect it will be the same for the time of the stage collapse."

"And I checked with the warden where your captor is being held. He's had no communication from anyone and, as you know, his brother died the day you were rescued. I have people checking for relatives who might hold a grudge," Ryder advised.

Selene collapsed against the back of her chair, anger escaping her like air from a burst balloon. "I'm sorry. I didn't mean to challenge what you're all doing."

"You have every right to know," Robbie said, his tone so understanding and tender that it made her throat choke up with emotion.

Busboys arrived at that moment with their appetizers, surprising Selene since Bart generally was the one who brought out her meal. She glanced back in his direction and considered him, trying to get a read on the man. He seemed slightly nervous and as his gaze met hers for a hot second, he quickly looked away.

"Thank you for all that you're doing," she said once the busboys had departed, leaving them to their meals.

Although the food at Alberto's was generally delicious, she had no appetite and everything she put in her mouth tasted like cardboard.

She barely ate half of her appetizer and didn't do much better after her frutti di mare arrived.

Robbie leaned close and whispered, "I won't ask if you're okay because you're not. But you need to eat something and keep up your strength."

Forcing a smile, she nodded and mouthed, "I will. Thanks."

She forced down the shrimp, but the thought of the clams and calamari—normally favorites of hers—turned her off tonight. Instead, she grabbed a piece of the focaccia.

The yeasty bread combined with the cheesy topping was welcome, even homey.

That feeling again.

She wanted to go home with Robbie. Have Lily meet her at the door with her bark, excited jumps and sloppy licks.

And those thoughts, that feeling, restored some of her appetite and she snatched up another piece of the focaccia and ate.

SELENE HAD THE tiniest hint of a smile on her face as she chewed, relieving some of Robbie's worry about her state of mind.

But who could blame her for being angry and troubled by what was happening?

He finished his delicious chicken parmigiana. Ryder and Sophie had likewise finished their meals.

A busboy arrived and asked Selene, "Do you need a box for that?"

She shook her head. "No, thanks. You can take it away," she said. The table was quickly cleared of their plates and the remnants of the bread basket.

Bart finally returned to the table, pad in hand. "Can I get you any dessert or coffee?" he said, although his demeanor broadcast that he hoped they would soon be gone.

"Nothing for me," Selene said and the others around the table echoed it. Well, all except for Ryder who said, "There's one thing I'd like."

Bart expelled an impatient breath. "What would that be?"

"Some pages from that notepad," Ryder said with a flip of his hand in its direction.

Bart shook his head, confused. "What? I don't get it."

Ryder reached into a jacket pocket and held up his badge. "I'd like a few pages from your notepad," he repeated.

Bart shook his head. "No. No way. I haven't done anything," he blurted out and gazed at Selene. "Are you okay with this?"

Selene's lips firmed into a tight line. "It would be better if you just did as he asked, Bart."

"She's right, Bart. Otherwise, I may have to take you down to our offices—"

Bart silenced Ryder by tearing out several sheets of paper from his notepad and almost tossing them at the CBI agent.

"I'll have the busboy bring over your check," he said and almost ran from the table.

"Well, he's not a happy camper," Robbie said facetiously.

Sophie jabbed a finger in his direction. "Don't underestimate what he'll do if he's our man," she warned.

He snagged her finger and playfully tugged on it. "I won't. He's not going to hurt either Selene or me again."

"Sophie's right. He's escalating so we all have to be on high alert," Ryder said as he took nitrile gloves from his jacket, picked up the notepad pages, and tucked them into an evidence bag.

The busboy arrived with the check and Robbie grabbed the waiter's wallet, reviewed the bill and then handed it back with his credit card.

When the busboy returned with the credit card slip, Robbie quipped, "What kind of tip should I leave?"

"Robbie," Sophie said in a warning tone that said she didn't like his joking.

"Okay, twenty percent it is," he said, not intimidated by his sister's motherly chastising.

He quickly filled out the slip and signed it. Then they went back to the condo so Ryder could collect the birthday card for the handwriting specialists.

As he had before, Ryder slipped on gloves to preserve any touch DNA and slipped the birthday card into an evidence bag.

"I'll rush the analysis, but it still may take a couple of days," he warned as Sophie and he stood at the door, ready to make their exit.

Selene laid a hand on his sleeve. "Whatever you can do would be appreciated, Ryder. Thank you."

Ryder offered her a smile and hug. Sophie did the same a second later but held on to Selene a little longer. A little tighter. "You're family now. We protect our family."

"I appreciate that," Selene said and embraced Sophie again.

Once they'd left with a series of good-bye barks from Lily, Robbie said, "We should take her for a long walk. She's been cooped up and pitties can be active."

Selene narrowed her gaze as she glanced down at the dog. "Do you think it's safe?"

"Whoever is doing this has escalated, but it's been my experience that even they need a breath to figure out what's next and we do too."

"Then I'm game and I'm sure Lily would love the fresh air," she said and grabbed the pittie's leash.

"But just in case... Do you have a baseball cap?" he asked.

She nodded, opened the door to a nearby foyer closet and pulled out a Rockies cap that she jauntily jammed on her head.

He winced and said, "The Rockies? Really?"

"Yes, why? Who do you root for?" she asked and made a point of tucking up as much of her hair as she could beneath the edges of the cap.

"The Mets. I love a challenge," he teased and grinned.

"I would have thought the Marlins since you live in Miami," she said as they headed out the door and to the elevator.

"My parents worked for the NSA, so we grew up in the D.C. area. But I always connected with underdogs like the Mets. Imagine living in the shadow of the Yankees," he explained.

SELENE UNDERSTOOD LIVING in the shadows quite well. It seemed that she'd lived in the shadows for a good part of her life.

"I get it," she said as they entered the elevator and rode down to the lobby.

Robbie dipped his head and considered her as the elevator began to move. "Care to share?"

With a hunch of her shoulders, she said, "When we were growing up, Rhea's talent was hard to ignore, even at an early age. She became so successful so young while I just...never found my footing."

He cradled her cheek, offering comfort. "We don't all develop at the same time and you're just as talented but in a different way."

"I know, and Rhea was always so supportive. She always believed in me even when I refused to and let my ex belittle me," she admitted.

"You're out of the shadows now, Selene. Everyone can see how special you are," he said and brushed a kiss against her lips.

She leaned into the kiss, wanting more, but the ding and slight dip of the elevator warned they'd reached the lobby.

Robbie tucked his hand into hers and together they strolled through the lobby and onto the street.

"Why don't we go toward the capitol?" she said and at his nod, they turned away from the pedestrian mall and strolled in silence toward the capitol building. It was a few blocks away and they enjoyed a night that had a little chill but was otherwise clear and bright.

Selene cherished the quiet moments with him even though it was clear he was on high alert despite his earlier words that her stalker would likely not attack again that day. She was vigilant also, watching for anything that seemed out of the ordinary.

Luckily, their walk was without incident and because of that, calm filled her as they entered the condo. She yanked off her ball cap and unleashed Lily, who seemed to feel the same way.

The pittie followed them to the couch and with a happy exhale, settled in at their feet.

With an equally contented sigh, Selene snuggled into Robbie's side on the sofa. "That was nice. Almost normal. I haven't had a lot of that in my life."

"Me either," Robbie admitted, surprising her.

Shifting slightly to see his face, she said, "Why not?"

A quick shift of his shoulders was followed by a suddenly serious look on his face. "With our parents in the NSA, they sometimes had to work long hours when we were little. It got better as we became teens, but by that time Sophie and I were already white hat hackers. When our gaming apps took over, we suddenly had more money than we could imagine and decided to join our cousins in Miami."

"And that was all she wrote? You were busy on all these cases?" she pressed, trying to gauge if he liked his life.

A crooked grin lifted his lips. "We were, and it's rewarding to make a difference. I love what we do and that we're doing it with family."

"Family's important," she said, grateful that Rhea and she were close and had been virtually adopted by the Gonzalez and Whitaker families.

"It is and I'm glad you're part of the family now as well," he said and his grin broadened, blue eyes glittering as he focused on her.

"I like it too," she said and shifted so that she was sitting on his lap, facing him. "Does that make us kissing cousins?" she teased, liking how she felt around him.

He made a face and said, "Not sure we're cousins but I like the part about kissing."

She laughed and cradled his face in her hands, careful to avoid his bruised cheek. His skin was slightly rough against her palms with the sandpaper of an evening beard.

Brushing her thumbs across his cheeks, she leaned in and whispered, "I think I'd like it too."

Chapter Fifteen

Take it slow, Robbie thought. *Real slow*, he reminded himself as she leaned in and finally kissed him.

Her lips were soft and had a slight chill from the night air but warmed quickly as they kissed over and over.

He splayed his hands across her back and drew her closer, her breasts pressed tightly to his chest. Her center covered his hardening length and heat built, dragging a low moan from him.

She did a little jump and broke from the kiss. Her gaze locked on his and she licked her lips, her hesitation clear in her electric blue eyes, now a dark cerulean.

He offered her a sad smile and slid his hand around to gently brush his fingers across her cheek. Softly he said, "I know this is…complicated."

A rough laugh escaped her, and she shook her head and dropped her gaze, unable to face him. Face what they had begun and seemingly wouldn't continue.

Placing his thumb and forefinger beneath her chin, he applied gentle pressure to urge her to meet his gaze once again. "I know you've been hurt in the past. Badly. But I would never hurt you or demean you in any way. I think you know that—in here," he said and slipped his hand down to lay it over her heart.

Selene laid her hand over his, bit her lower lip again and, with a shaky dip of her head, whispered, "I know."

Robbie turned his hand over to hold hers, and with a bounce of their joined hands against her thigh, he said, "I just want to hold you for a little bit. Is that okay?"

SELENE COULDN'T FIND the air to speak, her chest and throat tight with emotion.

She only nodded and settled in against him, her head tucked just beneath his chin. Her thighs cradled his hips where his erection nestled at her center.

That hardness and his moan had jolted her, not because of his rising passion, but because of her own. It had been so long since she'd wanted a man. But she wanted a physical relationship with this courageous and caring man.

Until the fear had rushed in and with it the memories of her husband belittling her and her kidnappers abusing her physically and mentally. That had brought back hesitation about being with a man.

But Robbie isn't just any man, the little voice in her head said.

Enveloped in his presence, with his arms wrapped around her, tender and protective, it was hard to deny that.

She lightly ran her hand across his chest—back and forth, back and forth—almost as if to comfort him, but in truth it was to comfort herself. To reassure herself of his stability and strength. Of the peace he had provided in the turmoil that had enveloped her once again.

He soothed his hand down her back and whispered, "Relax, mi amor. It's going to be fine, I promise."

My love, he'd said. How she wished that could be true.

Shifting back slightly and locking her gaze on his, she said, "What if I'm never right, Robbie? What if this broken woman is all that's left of me?"

A sad smile slipped across his face, and he once again brushed his fingers down her cheek.

"Have you ever heard of *kintsugi*?" he asked.

She shook her head, and he continued, mimicking the act of someone piecing something together as he spoke. "It's the Japanese practice of fixing a broken piece of pottery with gold lacquer."

A picture came to mind of some vases that Rhea had once had in the shop. "I've seen some pottery like that. They were beautiful."

The smile on his face brightened and he cradled her jaw. "Sometimes the repaired piece is even more beautiful than the original. Stronger. That's you, Selene. You are my strong and beautiful warrior."

She choked back a sob but then it was like a dam breaking and she was sobbing in his arms, her head buried against his chest.

He just held her, soothed her with softly murmured words she didn't really hear, lost in her pain but also hopefulness.

A second later, a rough bump came against her upper arm followed by a bark.

Lily seemed to be offering her support as well. Selene sat back and glanced at the pittie who had jumped up on the sofa.

"I'm okay," she said and rubbed Lily's head, letting her know that all was right with her.

And it was. If she was that broken pottery made whole again, Robbie was the potter, carefully piecing her back together with something more precious than gold. With love.

"Thank you," she said and rose to drop a watery and salty kiss on his lips.

When she slipped back onto his thighs, he cupped her cheeks with his hands and wiped away the remnants of her tears with his thumbs.

"You should try and get some rest. I have some more work

to do," he said and gestured to his knapsack as it sat by the dining table.

"I don't want to be alone. Would it bother you if I lay here and put a movie on?" she asked.

ROBBIE COULD NORMALLY work through anything but having her near would be tough since all he wanted to do was hold her close and help heal some of her pain. Only she could truly put all the final pieces of herself back in place.

But he lied and said, "Not a problem. Nothing bothers me when I get into a case."

He hauled out his laptop from his knapsack and found a message from his cousin Mia waiting for him.

John located several cameras along both the southern and northern routes the unsub took. Some video and screen grabs are attached along with possible locations where the unsub left 16th Street to go in other directions, she wrote.

Thanks, Mia. This is a big help, he replied and immediately downloaded all the files.

Unfortunately, much like the fifth man had done backstage at the bar, the man fleeing the scene of the stage collapse had on a baseball cap and a denim jacket whose collar was turned up to hide his face, as if aware there might be CCTV cameras in the area that would capture his features.

But he was pretty certain that the man leaving the bar was the same as the man in the general vicinity of the condo immediately after he'd been attacked. The baseball cap and denim jacket were similar, although the unsub had worn a hoodie beneath the jacket on the night he'd been attacked. Possibly for additional disguise or because it had been chillier that night.

The logo on the ball cap kept pulling him in, but none of the photos or videos provided a complete view of it to possibly give him a clue. It might take some splicing and joining to possibly make a better image and that would take time.

Because of that, he turned his attention to the videos that Mia's tech guru husband, John Wilson, had prepared. Wilson had done a great job of giving him the best samplings from several spots along 16th Street.

Thanks to that, he had screenshots of their unsub passing by several storefront doors. While there was no real standard for commercial doors, the most popular height was eighty inches. Based on that, he guesstimated their unsub was about five foot eleven, give or take. But Sophie and he had created an AI-based program that would give a more accurate reading and an approximation of the unsub's weight.

Their program was already in use by several companies that did custom tailoring for people who were unable to visit the shop to provide measurements.

Running the program across the various screenshots he'd made, it came back within seconds to confirm his guesstimate of the unsub's height and also indicated that based on the photos, he was approximately 175 pounds.

He tipped his chair back as he mulled that weight in light of the general body sizes of their three top suspects.

An average five-foot-eleven-inch male weighed two hundred pounds. At 175 pounds, their unsub was on the leaner side and might even look thin if they had more muscle and higher bone density.

In his mind's eye, he pictured Bart who was about six feet but thicker through the body.

While Bart had left a sour taste in his mouth, Robbie's initial thought was to eliminate him based on the general physical description gleaned from the videos.

That left recording studio Jason and bar security Ralph.

Based on the physical alone, Jason remained a viable unsub.

As for Ralph, he hadn't spent enough time with him to get a good sense of his height and weight.

Robbie vaguely remembered that Ralph and he were of the

same height, roughly six feet. So based on height, he couldn't eliminate him. Ralph had mostly been on the move during the few times they'd been together.

Closing his eyes and rocking a little on the chair legs, he tried to remember those moments and it occurred to him that Ralph had an average build that fit their unsub.

Muttering a curse, he dropped back onto all four chair legs, startling Selene, who had been watching a movie, and Lily, who hopped up onto all fours and barked at him in warning.

"Easy girl," he said and held his hand out to call the pittie over.

Lily raced over and he rubbed her head and body, earning sloppy doggy kisses as she excitedly laid her front paws on his thighs to reach his face.

"Down, girl. Down," he said and the pittie immediately obeyed, making him grateful for whoever had done such a good job of training her before having to leave her at the shelter.

Lily immediately responded and hurried back to Selene's side. *Another good sign*, Robbie thought.

Pitties were known to be protective and the fact that she had bonded with Selene and stayed close to her brought relief that if it was ever needed, Lily would respond.

Which made him think about what else they could teach Lily. Would she be able to attack if needed? Maybe even seek and find?

SHE HADN'T KNOWN Robbie all that long, but she could already recognize that—despite his playful moment with Lily—something was bothering him.

"Is everything okay?" she asked.

Robbie nodded. "It is. I have a little more info on the unsub's height and weight but not enough to rule out Jason or Ralph."

Selene narrowed her gaze as she contemplated what his analysis had said. "But you ruled out Bart?"

Robbie blew out a disgusted breath and angrily shook his head. "The guy may annoy me but based on my initial analysis, he's too big and too heavy."

"And that bothers you?" she asked, just to be sure.

He nodded. "I don't like the vibes I get from him, mostly because I don't like the way he looks at you."

She shouldn't like that he was jealous of Bart but was hard-pressed not to like that Robbie was annoyed by the other man's attentions. For far too long in her life, no man had cared enough to be bothered or jealous.

"He's just a waiter I know. Nothing more. I think you understand that, right?" she said, wanting him to know that he was the only man she had any interest in.

A crooked grin erupted on his face. "I know, mi amor."

He'd said it again: *my love*. Those simple words filled her with peace and contentment.

"Are you almost done for the night? It's late," she said and did a glance at her watch to confirm. Almost midnight.

"I am, except… Would you mind possibly training Lily to do a few more things?" he asked, dark brows scrunched low in question over his bright blue eyes.

"Like what?" she asked, thinking that Lily had already proven herself to be an obedient dog.

"Maybe seek and find. Possibly even attack to protect you," he said hesitantly, as if aware she might hesitate about the attack part.

Lily, as if sensing she was the topic of their conversation, swiveled her head back and forth between them, tracking their discussion.

With a quick motion of her hand, she commanded Lily up onto the sofa with her and rubbed the dog's head, worried about turning such a friendly animal into something else.

Her hesitation spoke volumes and Robbie reluctantly said, "How about just the 'seek and find' part? It might be a fun way for you to play with her."

It might, especially when it was just the two of them once Robbie went back to Miami. The thought of him leaving brought immense sadness and in response, Lily whined, in tune with her emotions.

"It's all right, girl. We'll have fun together," she said, and Robbie likewise immediately understood.

"You're thinking about the after, aren't you? About when I go back to Miami?" he pressed.

With a shrug, she said, "I have to think about that. Your life is in Miami and for now, my life is here."

"But the producer who's interested in you is in Miami. Would you leave your life here if she signed you?"

It was hard to think about leaving Rhea, especially when she was about to become a mother. Selene had already pictured herself being a doting aunt since she'd never imagined herself in another relationship and having a child.

But for a chance to follow her dreams, she would do it, hard as it might be to leave her family.

"I would. What about you? Have you ever considered leaving Miami?" she asked and held her breath as she waited for his answer.

It came immediately and without hesitation. "I would for the right reasons."

And as his gaze locked with hers, she knew without a doubt that she was one of those reasons.

"Down, Lily," she said to urge the dog to the floor so she could rise from the sofa.

Once she had stood, she held her hand out to Robbie. "Time for bed. Would you stay with me tonight?"

Chapter Sixteen

Robbie's gut clenched at the thought of lying beside her. Making love to her.

"Are you sure, Selene? I don't want to rush you," he said as he stood and walked to stand before her, hands jammed into his pockets to keep from taking her hand since he worried it might be too soon.

"I've never been more sure, Robbie," she said and wiggled her hand up and down to urge him to take it.

He jerked his hand from his pocket and slid it into hers.

With a tug, she led him toward her bedroom, Lily tagging along behind them.

As they neared the door, Robbie softly said, "Down, Lily."

Lily seemed to hesitate, ears slightly perked up as she looked from him to Selene, but then she lay down by the bedroom door.

"Good girl," he said to reinforce her actions before Selene and he entered the room and he closed the door behind them.

With another tug, she led him toward the bed but as they neared, worry that this was happening too fast punched him in the gut.

She eyed him, a question in her deep blue gaze.

He cradled her face in both his hands, willing her to understand. "I don't want to rush you."

"Because you're worried I'm not really ready for this?" she said, head tipped to one side as she examined his features.

Before he could say a word, she jumped in with, "I recall someone who called me his strong warrior."

With a huffed breath, he caressed her cheeks with his thumbs and said, "I did. You're strong and beautiful."

"Then show me."

A groan erupted from deep in his gut because it was impossible to refuse her.

But he intended to take it slow to give her a chance to change her mind.

Leaning in, he kissed her gently. Tenderly, she answered him, meeting his lips again and again. Opened to him so he could taste her sweetness.

He shifted his hands to her back and drew her near, all her delectable softness against his hard body. But as she wrapped her arms around him and held him tight, he flinched in pain.

A surprising curse exploded from her, and she said, "I'm sorry. I hurt you."

With a reluctant nod, he said, "I'm a little sore."

"Let me see," she said, and before he could stop her, she was drawing his T-shirt up and over his head, exposing his bruised back to her.

"Oh, my God, Robbie. I'm so sorry," she said and lightly ran her fingertips along his back, her touch electric against the bruises but also exploding his passion despite the pain.

He turned, snared her hands, and urged them to his chest. "I'm not sorry. I'd do it again in a second if it would always lead us here. To us being together."

WITH A QUICK bob of her head, Selene explored the muscled contours of his chest and lower, across the defined muscles of his abdomen.

He was lean but powerful. She skimmed the back of her

hands across all that muscle and he stood there, letting her explore. He was holding back passion, she knew. He wanted her to be ready and she was.

It had been too long since she'd known tenderness or passion. She didn't doubt that Robbie could show her both. That he could also show her love.

"Touch me, Robbie. Please," she pleaded and slipped her hands to the metal button of his jeans. Shakily she undid them and was about to work on the zipper when he slipped his hands down to stop her.

"Slow," he said and urged her hands back up to his chest as he raised his hands and cupped her breasts, caressing them until she was swaying toward him and kissing him again.

The kisses intensified as their caresses grew bolder and harder until with a rough breath, Robbie broke their kiss and trailed his lips down to the crook of her neck and shoulder. A tender love bite had her shaking and holding onto his shoulders as her knees weakened.

She keened a plea for more and he sucked that sensitive spot, each draw of his mouth making her insides clench with need.

Covering him, she stroked his length until it wasn't enough, and she had to have his skin against her.

In a flurry, she slid beneath his briefs to caress him.

He groaned, the sound vibrating through her as his body also shook from the desire driving them.

That sound and the feel of him, so hot and hard in her hand, undid them.

TAKING IT SLOW was impossible, Robbie thought as he eased his hands beneath the hem of her T-shirt and drew it up and over her head.

The bra she wore was white cotton with the barest hint of

lace along the cups. So simple and yet it couldn't be sexier to him because it was so Selene.

He reached behind, undid the clasp and her full breasts spilled free. Cupping them, he ran his thumbs across the tight tips and said, "You are so beautiful, mi amor."

Stepping closer, she said, "I want to feel you against me, my love."

Sliding his hands to her back, he urged her near and had to fight back a groan. Her softness, fullness, felt so right against him.

A second later, they were both yanking at their jeans to remove them and just as quickly, Selene was sitting on the edge of the bed, urging him to join her.

He stood in the gap between her legs, but he kneeled, bringing himself face to face with her. Letting him bend and kiss her breasts. Suckle them as she held him close, and she moaned with pleasure.

Her thighs, as she cradled him between her legs, trembled from her growing passion and Robbie wanted to take her over. Wanted to please her before he sought his release.

Dropping lower, he kissed her center and she nearly jumped off the edge of the bed.

He kept her close, his hands around her thighs as kiss after kiss drew her ever upward until with a hoarse shout of his name, she climaxed.

SELENE'S WORLD WAS a whirl of satisfaction and need at the same time.

She gripped his buttocks, wanting him inside, but he pulled away for a second with a rushed, "Protection."

When he returned, he eased between her legs once more and soothed her with gentle strokes of her thighs as she felt him at her center.

His gaze locked with hers, almost in question, but she answered by rising to kiss him and guide him with a loving stroke of her hand.

She sucked in a breath and followed his gaze down, marveling at their joining. Celebrating that union as he filled her and held still, embracing that very special first between them.

Her body trembled with his possession and beneath her hands, his body did the same as he threw his head back, eyes closed. Lips pursed tight against the sensations buffeting him as much as they were her.

But as her heartbeat sounded loudly in her ears, he moved, and she nearly came undone with that first slow stroke.

She grabbed hold of his shoulders and moaned. Pleaded for more with the shift of her hips. He answered, shifting in and out of her. With one last powerful stroke, the world exploded around her again.

His rough groan and his soft sigh of her name said that he had also found his pleasure.

He held himself inside her, savoring the remnants of her climax, kissing her as they both drifted back and their heartbeats slowed.

When he started to slip out of her, he said, "I'll be back."

He hurried away from her and to the bathroom where she heard the rush of water before he came back with a damp washcloth. Tenderly he cared for her before tossing the washcloth on the pile of his clothes and urging her beneath the covers.

She patted the space beside her. "Come to bed, my love."

He grinned that crooked boyish grin that did all kinds of things to her heart and then he slipped beneath the covers. Tucking her tight to him, her back against his front, he laid a possessive arm around her waist, dropped a kiss on the side of her face and whispered, "Sleep tight, mi amor."

ROBBIE WAS AWAKE long after the softening of Selene's body and her deep regular breaths confirmed she had fallen asleep.

His mind was too busy reviewing what he'd spotted in the videos and what little he knew of both Jason and Ralph. Neither had struck him as dangerous—although there had been that one tiny moment when it seemed like a curtain had opened on Jason's features and shown him a different side.

His sister Sophie might have warned him that jealousy was coloring his perspective and that might be true. But as far as he was concerned, Jason was number one on his short list of suspects.

Satisfied with that, he finally released his mind to sleep, but he was in that blurry world of half-sleep when Selene did a startled jump against him.

Suddenly she was thrashing and moaning, clearly in the throes of a nightmare. She flailed her fists and nailed him on his bruised cheek, dragging a pained grunt from him.

To protect both of them, he gently grasped her arms, but that only worsened the situation.

She fought him, rolling her body from side to side as if trying to escape and let out a scream.

Outside the door, Lily began barking and pawing the door, aware that something was wrong.

"Selene, amor. Por favor, wake up," he crooned to her softly and tempered his hold, trying to be gentle.

Selene jerked awake, her gaze frantically searching his face and the room, almost as if she didn't know where she was. Frantic, harsh breaths erupted from her along with an anguished moan.

Robbie released one of her arms and cradled her cheek, urging her to meet his gaze. "Amorcito, it's Robbie. You're safe here. You're safe," he said, wanting to pull her out of the nightmare and back to reality.

Little by little her gaze grew more focused and as she finally acknowledged him, a strained cry escaped her. "I'm so sorry. I hit you. I hit you," she repeated over and over.

"Sssh, mi amor. You were having a nightmare," he said and passed his thumb tenderly over her lips to quiet her.

She buried her head against his chest and wrapped her arms around him.

He rocked her to comfort her until her breaths were more regular and her body had lost her earlier fight and tension.

When he thought she was ready, he said, "Do you want to share?"

She violently shook her head. "No. I don't want that part of my life touching any part of what we have."

He didn't want to state the obvious, namely that it already had, but didn't press.

He was a patient man, and he could wait until she was ready to talk about her nightmare. But it did worry him that the beautiful lovemaking they'd shared earlier that night had somehow been responsible for bringing back painful memories.

As she drifted off to sleep in his arms once again, he vowed to do whatever he could to bring her nothing but joy instead of pain.

Chapter Seventeen

Robbie left their bed just as the first rays of sunlight were leaking past the edges of the curtains in her room.

She heard him picking up his clothes from the floor and softly padding to the door. Lily barked as he exited and as he closed the door behind him, she heard him commanding the dog to be quiet.

The hiss of water through pipes said he was showering, and she imagined the water streaming across his broad shoulders and down his bruised back.

He'd been hurt because of her multiple times, including when she'd smacked him in the face the night before.

Pain sprung up beneath her breastbone and she laid a hand there to will it away while promising herself that she would do whatever it took for him not to be hurt again.

But was it a promise that she could keep?

His murmured words of comfort and support filtered through her brain.

You're my strong warrior.

I am, last night's nightmare notwithstanding.

It was one she hadn't had in months but with everything that had been going on over the last few days, her control had slipped, and she'd let the past come alive again.

Another thing she wouldn't let happen once more.

Armed with that conviction, she rose, showered and got ready to face the day.

When she exited her room, Lily excitedly raced in her direction and hopped up, demanding her attention. The earthy aroma of coffee spiced the air and Robbie was at the dining table, looking fresh and alert even though he'd probably only gotten a few hours of sleep.

She walked over and as she did so, he swiveled his chair, inviting her to sit on his lap.

She did and kissed him, offering her love and hopefully an apology for what had happened during her nightmare.

"How are you feeling?" he asked, his gaze a stormy gray instead of his usual aqua blue.

"Happy that you're here," she said and stroked her fingers through the shower-damp strands of his hair.

"Good to hear," he said and then quickly added, "I've sent the team what I worked on last night. Hopefully, they can confirm the decision I reached about Bart and do a deep dive into Jason and Ralph."

She inhaled deeply and shook her head. "It's just hard to believe it's one of them—and why now?"

With a hunch of his shoulders, he said, "Who knows? But by the time we're done, we will know. And if it's someone else, we'll know that too."

He said it with such certainty that she didn't doubt that he and his team would do exactly what he said.

A ping on her phone warned her of a text message. She pulled her phone out of her back pocket and read aloud the message from Jason.

E-mailed you the file for the producer. The song is a hit. Will miss you when you go to Miami.

She held the phone up for Robbie to see. "Does that sound like the text message from a man who would want to hurt me?"

With a wave of his hands, he said, "Stranger things have happened. Evil is good at hiding."

Lily whined and went to the front door, obviously warning that she needed to go.

"Do we have time to walk her and maybe grab breakfast?" she asked and slipped off his lap.

"We do. Sophie is going to text when the contractor gets to the bar, and we'll go over to see about the repairs. It'll also give me some time to get a better perception of Ralph," he said, then stood and tucked her hand into his.

At the door, she leashed Lily, and in no time, they were at the front door of the condo building.

Robbie sidled past her to walk out the door and make sure all was safe before she followed him out.

They headed in the direction of the bar and recording studio, vigilant as they walked to make sure they weren't being followed.

Nothing seemed out of the ordinary and just a few short blocks away, Robbie directed her toward a nearby café that had outdoor seating so that Lily could stay with them.

The waitress quickly seated them at a table close to the café's front windows and away from the pedestrians strolling by along the street. Lily lay quietly at their feet and the waitress brought over a small bowl with some water and a doggy biscuit for the pittie.

As the waitress handed them menus, Selene said, "Thanks so much."

The waitress, who was barely out of her teens, grinned and said, "I just love puppies."

"She's a good pup," Selene said. She reached down and rubbed Lily's head.

"I'll be back to take your orders and bring some coffee,"

she said and hurried away to take menus to another couple at the far side of the outdoor patio.

Robbie took only a quick look at the menu, more interested in keeping an eye on what was going on around them to make sure Selene was safe.

As he'd told her yesterday, while her stalker's actions were escalating, he expected that their unsub needed a moment to regroup and plan their next attack.

Sadly, he had no doubt there would be another attack.

When the waitress returned a few minutes later, she poured coffee for both of them and Selene placed her order for the French toast while he stayed basic with eggs, hash browns, bacon and toast.

Selene grabbed some sugar packets for her coffee and Robbie did the same. "Will you be sending the producer the files today?" he asked as he added the sugar to his coffee and topped it off with a lot of cream.

"I want to do another listen when we get home, just in case. Then I'll send them," she said and stirred her coffee.

"The producer would be a fool to turn you down," he said, having been impressed by what he'd heard in both the recording studio and during her performance.

She offered him a smile and sipped her coffee. "Thank you but you're probably not impartial."

He grinned and nodded. "I'm not. I'd like nothing better than for you to come to Miami."

His words filled her with joy and hopefulness. "I'd like that too. Believe it or not, I've never been there."

That launched him into a rundown of all the wonderful places and foods he'd show her in his adopted hometown and in truth, it all sounded interesting but also very different from her life in Colorado.

"It sounds exciting, and I'd love to meet your cousins in person," she said just as the waitress brought over their meals.

Silence reigned as hunger took over. She dove into the tasty French toast topped with strawberry compote.

When their food had arrived, Lily had come to her feet, expecting a treat, and Selene didn't disappoint, cutting off a piece of her French toast and feeding it to her.

"She'll get fat if you keep that up," Robbie teased, a lopsided grin on his face.

"We'll just have to exercise her more," she said, imagining that in the future they'd be able to spend more time together.

His grin broadened into a wide, welcoming smile. "We will. There's a great walking trail near my condo in Miami."

Miami. A world away from Denver and only if the producer agreed to sign her. "That sounds like fun," she said and as she ate, she pictured them strolling beneath shady palms with Lily.

They had just finished their meals and were paying when Robbie got a text message.

After a quick peek at his phone, Robbie said, "Sophie is at the bar and the contractor is already at work."

"I don't know how to thank you for arranging all that. But the cost—"

"Is nothing you have to worry about, Selene. You're family," he said yet again and as his gaze locked on hers, she knew better than to argue.

"Thank you," she said. When Robbie rose and held out his hand, she tucked hers into it and grabbed Lily's leash for the short walk to the bar.

It was impossible to miss the sounds of hammering and saws whirring as they neared the bar. A bright yellow sign at the door advised that the restaurant was closed.

For how long? Selene wondered as Robbie called his sister to let her know they'd arrived.

Barely a minute later, she opened the door, and the louder sounds of construction spilled onto the street.

The door closed behind them and a cacophony of noise assaulted them from the pounding and buzzing echoing throughout the space.

Sophie approached and pointed across the restaurant area to the hall leading to the security office and greenroom.

"Hopefully it's quieter there," she said in a loud voice to overcome the noise. She pushed off in that direction, expecting them to follow.

They did, hurrying through the empty space into the hall, bypassing security and going straight into the greenroom where Sophie closed the door behind them once they'd entered.

"QUE PASA, HERMANITA?" Robbie asked, wondering what was up with his sister.

"Contractor says he can finish repairs to the stage by Monday, but he found some rot in the areas beneath the restaurant. He says we were lucky to find it before anyone got hurt. That may take until next week to fix."

"What does the owner have to say about that?" Robbie asked, thinking that the owner couldn't be happy with the delay, though he ought to be grateful to avoid a bigger issue.

"Torn. He says he didn't know about the issues and is good with the fix but hates that the bar will be closed for a week," Sophie advised with a dubious shrug.

"You don't believe the not knowing part?" Robbie pressed, reading his sister's tone and features.

Sophie pointed in the direction of the kitchen. "I spoke to some of the staff who said they'd mentioned to Ralph that the floor felt soft and saggy."

"And I assume Ralph confirmed that he told the owner about the complaints?" Robbie said, tilting his head to the side in emphasis.

Sophie literally squirmed before his eyes and her gaze skipped from him to focus on Selene.

"How well do you know Ralph?" she asked.

With a slight lift of her shoulders, Selene said, "Not much really. He's good with the staff. Protective even. Fair. Responsible. Why?"

Sophie peered at him as she said, "Ralph didn't show up for work today and no one can reach him. Plus, our initial dive into his background has brought up some alarming info."

Selene's hand trembled in his as she swayed a little. He guided her to the well-worn sofa so she could sit with Lily draped across her feet, offering comfort.

"What kind of info?" Selene asked in a soft voice that was barely audible over the noise of construction.

Sophie hesitated but Robbie implored her to continue with a sharp look.

With a nod, Sophie launched into her report. "Ralph served time for breaking and entering when he was eighteen. But what's alarming are a few arrests for assault about ten years ago. His wife was the victim."

Beside him, Selene shivered but then straightened her back, finding inner strength. "That's hard to believe. Like I said before, around here Ralph has been fair, and you saw how protective he was with Scott."

"Maybe you've only seen one side of him," Sophie countered, although her tone was almost apologetic.

"You said ten years ago, Soph. People can change, right?" Robbie said, worried about Ralph's background but also in agreement with Selene's assessment based on what he'd seen of the man so far.

"They can, Robbie. But it warrants additional investigation," his sister replied with a warning tone.

"We can do that. What about Jason? Anything on him?" he said since the studio owner had rubbed him the wrong way.

Sophie eyed him intently. "Nothing so far."

"But you'll keep on searching?" he challenged with the arch of a brow.

"The team will keep on searching," Sophie confirmed with a dip of her head.

Selene piped in with, "Does that make sense? If you didn't find anything at first—"

"Sometimes the truth is buried deep," Robbie said. He squeezed her hand to reassure her and then peered at his sister. "Can you send me the info on Ralph?"

Sophie nodded. "I'll e-mail it."

"Good. I think it's time I got Selene and Lily home," he said, then popped to his feet and walked to the door.

Selene and Lily followed, but at the door, his sister approached, eyed Selene and said, "Would you mind giving us a moment?"

Selene nodded and said, "Sure. I'll wait for you in the bar area."

Once she had walked away, Sophie laid a hand on his arm and said, "Don't let what you're feeling for her affect the case. You know how dangerous that can be."

"I know what I'm doing," he shot back.

"Do you? She's not your average woman," Sophie warned. It didn't take a genius to know what she meant. Most women didn't have the kinds of wounds that Selene carried with her every day.

"That's why I love her, Soph. She's amazing," he said, wanting more than anything to convince his sister that he was serious about Selene.

Sophie pursed her lips, took a deep breath and then nodded. "Keep her safe but keep yourself safe as well," she said and laid a hand over his heart.

"I will, but what about you and Ryder? Is he 'the one'?" he said, using air quotes in emphasis.

Joy glittered in aqua eyes, so much like his own, and she smiled. "He is, which makes my next decision a hard one. I'm not sure I'm going back to Miami."

He dipped his head as he thought about leaving without her. They'd been a team for so long that it made his heart hurt to consider it, but more than anything, he wanted his sister to be happy.

"No reason you can't work remotely, and Selene and I can visit a lot, especially once Rhea and Jax have their baby."

"You think Selene will leave her career here?" Sophie pressed, eyes narrowed as she considered him.

"A Miami producer is interested in her and I've heard her demo. She'd be a fool to not sign her."

"So I guess she's 'the one,'" his sister teased, mimicking his earlier air quotes.

"I think she is," he said and jerked a thumb in the direction of the bar area. "I should go drop her off at home. I want to go chat with Ralph's wife and Ralph if I can find him."

Sophie pointed an index finger into his chest. "Be safe."

He grabbed her finger and playfully shook it. "I will. Are you done here?"

She motioned toward the hall. "One camera left to connect and check and then I'm headed to the recording studio to meet Jason and the owner."

The thought of Jason with his sister made him uneasy. "Be careful with him. He's not what he seems."

"I'll keep that in mind, but remember—black belt," she said and mimicked some karate chops with her hands.

Grabbing her hands, he hauled her close for a tight hug. "Cuídate," he said, warning her to take care.

"Tú también," she said, asking him to do the same.

He skimmed a kiss across her cheek and then rushed out to join Selene where she waited in the bar area.

SELENE GLANCED BACK toward where Sophie stood in the hall, a worried frown on her face.

"Everything okay with you two?" she asked, hating that she might be causing a rift between the siblings.

"Everything's good. I'll take you and Lily home—"

"No. We're going with you," she said and as if to agree with her, Lily barked from her spot by her side.

Robbie pursed his lips and vehemently shook his head. "I don't think—"

She laid her index finger on his lips to stop him. "I'm not going to be a victim again. I want control over what's happening."

"It could be dangerous," he said, and it dragged an abrupt laugh from her.

"And it hasn't been so far?" she said, holding her hands out wide. "Look what happened here."

He rolled his eyes and wagged his head from side to side. "You win, but you have to stay close and keep Lily even closer."

"I don't think that will be a problem," she said and glanced down at the dog who was pressed tight to Selene's leg.

With a nod, Robbie pulled his phone from his pocket and after a few swipes, he said, "Ralph's address is nearby but his wife is in Littleton."

"That's not far from here. Maybe ten miles at most," Selene advised.

"I'd like to visit her first. I want to find out more about what happened," Robbie said and clasped Selene's hand.

"I can drive us there," she said. They hurried from the bar to a parking lot around the corner from the condo where Selene had parked her Jeep.

The air had gotten chillier during their walk and the sun had dimmed, warning that weather was on the way. If she was any judge of it, maybe another of those weird spring snows that came suddenly and left just as quickly.

"What's the address?" she asked as she started up the car.

Robbie read off the address in Littleton and Selene plugged it into her nav system. In no time they were driving along the city streets to access the highways for the twenty minute drive to the Denver suburb.

Selene was grateful when the heat in her Jeep kicked to life, driving away the chill in the air and in her gut, as the sky continued to darken to a leaden gray, worrying her.

She leaned forward to peer through the windshield at the angry clouds overhead. "It looks like snow again."

Beside her, Robbie shook his body and said, "Brrr. I am so not used to going from the 60s to snow."

Lily barked from the back seat where they'd harnessed her, as if in agreement.

Selene laughed but then someone in a bright red Bronco cut her off, forcing her to brake abruptly. She slowed, but the person braked hard again, obviously intentionally.

"Slow down and pull over," Robbie said, the worry evident in his tone and the way he braced his hands on the dash and door.

She did as he asked, but the Bronco mimicked her move. Its brake lights flashed angry red again in challenge.

Robbie muttered a curse and was about to say something else when the Bronco suddenly flew off, riskily weaving in and out of traffic to put distance between them.

"Did you get a look at the driver?" he asked.

In truth, she had been so busy avoiding a collision that she hadn't noticed anything except the bright red brake lights ahead of her.

"No. Did you get the license plate number?" she asked as the nav system instructed her off Route 25 and onto Route 85.

Robbie nodded. "I did. I'm sending it to Ryder to check out," he said, fingers flying over the face of his smartphone.

The last ten miles flew by quickly and without incident and before long she was turning off the highway to reach Wolhurst Lake, where Ralph's ex-wife lived in a tidy mobile home close to the lake and not all that far from some woods that bordered the Platte River.

The mobile home was located in an age-restricted community with a variety of amenities for residents. The streets and homes were well kept as was the mobile home where Ralph's ex lived.

Selene parked the Jeep just as the first fat flakes of snow started coming down.

"Great," Robbie said as he exited the Jeep and walked to meet her on the stone path to the front door.

The small strip of grass by the street was just beginning to show spring green and the home boasted window boxes where winter pansies provided the first bits of seasonal color.

The door opened even before they reached it, almost as if his ex had been expecting a visit.

"Is it Ralph? Is he okay?" she asked, wringing her hands as her nervous gaze jumped from Selene to Robbie.

"Ralph is fine as far as we know. Do you mind if we come in?" Robbie said.

"Only if you show me your badge first," she said defiantly and tilted her head of salt-and-pepper hair up in challenge.

Chapter Eighteen

Robbie raised his hands. "We're not police. We just want to ask you a few questions."

"Please," Selene pleaded and that seemed to work some magic on the woman who stepped aside to let them enter.

The space inside the mobile home was comfortable and nicely put together. Custom woodwork and beams were offset by clean white walls and white oak flooring that ran through all the visible areas. Off to one side of the living room was a nice-sized kitchen with white cabinets and stainless-steel appliances that gleamed brightly.

"You have a nice home, Mrs. Emerson," he said and followed the older woman as she hurried past them and into the living room.

"Thank you, but why are you here? Is Ralph in some kind of trouble? He's not drinking again, is he?" she said and tucked her arms across her chest in challenge.

Robbie pointed his index finger at his chest as he said, "I'm Robbie Whitaker. I work with South Beach Security in Miami."

"You're a long way from Miami," Mrs. Emerson said with a huffed breath and a rebellious lift of her chin.

He kept a friendly tone and gestured to Selene and said, "This is Selene Reilly—"

"I've heard of you. Ralph has mentioned you often," his ex-wife said, her demeanor softening slightly.

"I perform at the bar where Ralph works. He's always been very helpful," Selene said with a warm smile that seemed to melt some of the woman's iciness.

"Then why are you here?" his ex-wife said.

"Do you mind if we sit, Mrs. Emerson?" he asked and gestured to the large brown sofa along the far wall of the living room.

"Patty. You can call me Patty," she said, her demeanor growing friendlier.

"Thank you, Patty," Selene said and took the lead, daintily sitting on the sofa and commanding Lily to sit.

Robbie joined her on the sofa and bent slightly to rub Lily's head. "We appreciate you talking to us, Patty. Someone has been trying to hurt Selene and we're trying to figure out who might be responsible."

Patty did a startled jump. "And you think Ralph has something to do with it?"

With a shrug, Robbie said, "We don't, but we have to eliminate all possibilities. What can you tell us about Ralph?"

Patty sat in a wing chair opposite them, knees primly tucked close, her hands clasped tightly. Her knuckles were white with pressure. "What can I say? He lost his way while we were married but he's straightened out his act."

"How do you know that?" Robbie asked, fighting not to sound accusatory.

With a quick shift of her shoulders and a pained look on her face, she said, "We've been seeing each other again."

A surprised inhale escaped Selene. "Even after—" she began, but Patty immediately cut her off.

"Yes, even after he hit me, Selene. I know you can't understand—"

"But I do. My husband mentally abused me and then I was physically abused by two other men," Selene admitted and that brought a rush of embarrassed color to Patty's neck and face.

"I'm sorry that happened to you, but Ralph and I..." She hesitated as tears came to her eyes and she looked away. Sucking in a deep breath, she held it and then the words rushed from her body. "We lost a child and Ralph started drinking. That's when he got violent. Never before. Never since."

Robbie couldn't imagine the pain of that loss and it didn't excuse Ralph's actions, but he couldn't help feeling sympathy for the older man. "We're so very sorry for your loss."

"Yes, we are. It couldn't have been easy," Selene said and reached across the space to lay a comforting hand on Patty's knee.

Patty offered Selene a sad smile and sniffle. "Thank you. You think the pain goes away but it never does. You understand that."

Selene nodded. "I do," she said without hesitation.

His heart ached for the two women, but he had no choice but to ask the next most obvious question. "Does Ralph still drink?"

Patty shook her head and wiped away her tears with a shaky hand. "After the last time they took him away for hitting me, Ralph promised me he'd stop drinking. He's been sober for the last ten years and about a year ago, we drifted together again."

Selene peered in his direction and said, "I think we have all we need. Don't you, Robbie?"

He nodded, stood and held his hand out to her. "I think we do."

Facing Patty, he forced a smile and said, "We appreciate you taking the time to chat with us."

"Whoever is trying to hurt you, I know in here that it isn't Ralph," she said and did a little cross over her heart.

Selene recognized the gesture well. It was one her Irish grandmother and mother had often done in mass and when making a promise.

"I believe you. He's been nothing but kind to me," Selene said. With a final hug, she hurried to her Jeep, Robbie hot on her heels.

When they reached the SUV, Robbie tugged her close and embraced her. Whispering in her ear, he said, "I'm sorry you still have that pain. I wish… I wish I could make it go away."

The barest hint of a smile slipped over her lips. "You do, my love. More than I ever thought possible."

She kissed him then and he answered, opening his mouth to hers. Kissing her over and over until they were both breathing heavily.

After they had pulled apart, he stroked his hand through her hair and cradled her skull, the gesture both protective and possessive. "I'm so sorry that the pain is still with you. I wish I could—"

She laid an index finger on his lips. They were still wet and warm from their kisses.

"You have already helped, Robbie. When I'm with you, I don't think about the past—only the future."

Replacing her index finger with her lips, she kissed him again to prove just how much he meant to her.

When they shakily broke away from the kiss, Robbie laid his forehead on hers and whispered, "I love you, Selene."

"I love you too," she said, feeling free to live and love for the first time in way too long.

The welcoming smile on his lips faded as he glanced toward her car and the snow that was still falling gently, coating everything with a blanket of white.

"We should go chat with Ralph before this weather gets any worse."

She hated the thought of confronting the other man. She

liked Ralph and he had always been a friend. But his violent past worried her. Had something made him slide from sobriety and make her the target of his anger?

As she went to walk to the driver's-side door, Robbie tugged her back and held out his hand for the keys. At her questioning look, he said, "I've taken a defensive driving class. Just in case that Bronco shows up again or the weather gets worse."

She handed him the keys, grateful for his intercession. The few short minutes with the Bronco's seeming road rage had unnerved her and it had taken all her concentration to avoid rear-ending the other vehicle. She wasn't sure she could do it with roads slick with new-fallen snow.

Once they were settled in the SUV, Robbie connected his phone, plugged in Ralph's address and pulled away from the curb to get back on the highway toward downtown Denver.

They traveled in silence for several minutes, the only sound the rhythmic thump of the windshield wipers clearing away the snow. They stayed vigilant for signs of the alarming red Bronco. Unfortunately, Broncos had become quite popular, and they spotted one or two red ones during the ride. Luckily, none had approached them.

They were turning off one highway to access the second one toward Denver when Robbie's phone rang.

"WHAT'S UP, RYDER?" Robbie asked as he answered the call.

"I've got some info on that Bronco for you," Ryder said.

Robbie tightened his hold on the wheel as he waited for Ryder's report. "Selene and I are ready. I've got you on speaker."

"The driver of that Bronco has filed various lawsuits where he claimed to be injured in a car accident," Ryder said.

"So he's staging the accidents to bilk the insurance company or driver to pay up?" Robbie said to confirm his understanding of the report.

"Definitely. I made a quick call to the district attorney and apparently, the driver may be part of an insurance fraud ring they're investigating. So you don't need to worry about him anymore," Ryder said. In the background, Robbie heard Sophie murmur something and then her voice came across the line.

"How did it go with Ralph Emerson's wife?"

"She cooperated and my gut tells me Ralph might not be our guy. But I'll let you know more once we talk to him," Robbie said.

"Whatever you do, stay safe," Sophie urged again. Selene laid a hand on his thigh and squeezed it as if to affirm Sophie's statement.

"We will. Do you have anything else on Jason?" he asked, still leaning toward the other man being a suspect despite any evidence to support that impression.

"Nothing criminal. But I've asked Trey to have the team run his personal and business financials. They might give us other clues," Sophie advised.

"That sounds good. Let us know once you have anything and we'll do the same," he said and after Sophie confirmed that she would, he ended the call.

"You're really focused on Jason being the stalker, aren't you?" Selene said and combed his hair back with her fingers so she could watch him as he answered. His hair was slightly damp from the snow that had melted in the heat of the SUV's cabin.

"I can't say why—"

"Can't you?" she challenged and leaned forward to fix her gaze on him.

"Yes, I'm a little jealous, but it's not that. I saw something... something that bothers me," he admitted and tapped his hands on the wheel as he tried to explain his gut reaction.

She slipped her fingers through his hair again and surprised him by saying, "I trust your gut, Robbie."

A relieved sigh escaped him as did the peace that followed her admission of support.

They flew the last few miles until they pulled up in front of the small apartment building on the fringes of downtown Denver. The area was one in transition where several of the nearby buildings were being renovated while others were looking decidedly rundown. Not even the icing of bright white snow could hide the grunge.

Ralph's condo was in that group that needed some love and care.

After parking a few doors down, they unharnessed Lily from the car and walked with her to Ralph's building. There were four old-fashioned buzzer buttons with lopsided metal nameplate holders. A handwritten name on yellowed paper advised that Ralph was in apartment 4A.

Robbie pressed the buzzer button and a few seconds later, a loud buzz and click unlocked the front door.

"Not much security," he said, then opened the door and stepped inside first to clear the area. Once he felt it was safe, he held his hand back to invite Selene to hold it.

The first floor had a small landing area with four brass mailboxes. The dated black-and-white tiles on the landing were scuffed but clean. Despite that, a musty smell permeated the small space as did the aroma of frying onions and garlic, probably from one of the tenants cooking a meal.

They walked up the four flights of stairs together, climbing to Ralph's floor. The walls were thin and the sounds of people chatting and television programs filtered into the stairway landings and halls as they hiked up the stairs.

On the fourth floor, they walked to the apartment at the end of the hall but as they neared, the door opened.

Ralph's large frame filled the doorway. His T-shirt stretched across thick muscle and bore various stains. His jeans button was undone, letting his bulging belly spill over the waistband.

Now that Robbie had a better look at the man, he realized that while Ralph was about the same height as their suspect, he was far beefier than what his program had indicated was the unsub's weight. But was that enough to eliminate him from their list?

Ralph's gaze seemed unfocused at first, but then he ran a hand through his hair to comb it into place and growled, "What do you want?"

Robbie had stopped several feet from the door, but even at that distance, he smelled the alcohol. "We just want to ask you a few questions."

Ralph grunted and then laughed a dry, cracked laugh. "I had nothing to do with it. Nothing."

"Have you been drinking again?" Selene asked in a soft, pleading voice.

Ralph shook his head and looked away. "No, but I was tempted," he admitted.

"Why do I smell alcohol?" Robbie challenged with an arch of a brow.

"Because I smashed the bottle. You're welcome to come in and see for yourself," he said, then stepped back and threw his arm out wide to invite them to enter.

Robbie hesitated but if Selene could trust his judgment on Jason, he had to have faith in Selene's belief in Ralph.

But he still went first and protectively pulled Selene behind him just in case.

He immediately saw the evidence that backed Ralph's claim that he'd smashed a bottle. A wet stain and dent marked one wall. At the base of that wall were the broken bits of a Jack Daniels bottle.

"Why were you tempted?" Selene asked in that soft, imploring tone again as Robbie and she sat on the sagging cushions of Ralph's couch with Lily parked protectively by her feet.

Ralph dragged a hand through his hair again and then down

across his beard, which rasped loudly in the small apartment. "The bar owner blames me for what happened. He thinks I shouldn't have let you investigate."

"He didn't fire you, did he?" Selene said, worry coloring her voice. Lily whined as she sensed Selene's upset and Selene calmed her with a soothing stroke of her head.

Ralph plopped into a seat across from them, the chair groaning and creaking from the abrupt deposit of his weight. "He threatened to fire me, but I reminded him that I'd warned him several times that the floor by the restaurant area was sketchy."

"And he was afraid you'd tell the contractor and inspectors that he ignored a dangerous condition," Robbie said, wanting to get a clear picture of what had happened.

Ralph nodded. "Yeah, that."

"Why the drink?" Robbie said and gestured toward the shattered liquor bottle.

Ralph expelled a harsh breath and held his hands out in pleading. "I felt like my life was spiraling out of control again and I'd worked so hard to rebuild it after… I'm not proud of what I did to Patty. She didn't deserve it. She was a good wife. A great mother."

"You always hurt the ones you love," Robbie said, trying to be understanding and sympathetic even though he didn't approve of what Ralph had done.

"I loved Patty. I still do. I'm lucky that she's willing to give me a second chance. I don't deserve it and I won't fail her again," Ralph said with certainty, strength and also immense sadness.

Robbie believed him. And it also convinced him that Ralph was not the man behind the attacks on Selene. Despite that, he had to press Ralph for more info.

"Would you mind providing a handwriting sample?" Robbie asked and Ralph immediately reached for a pad and pen on the coffee table, wrote a few words down, signed the sheet and then tore it off and passed it to Robbie.

"Thanks. Is there anyone at the bar who you think might want to hurt Selene?" Robbie pressed.

Pursing his lips, Ralph skipped his gaze across both of them and then shook his head. "No. Most everyone gets along. Well, almost everyone."

Selene seemed to know who didn't. "You mean Rachel, right?"

Ralph nodded. "Yeah, Rachel. She was pissed when you replaced her for the weekend slots and she had to become your backup."

"I knew she was upset, but I include her with all those duets we do," she said, clearly upset by Ralph's suspicions.

"Which only makes it worse because she knows she wouldn't do the same and that makes her even more bitter," Ralph pointed out.

Robbie had seen the other singer's attitude the other night, but their suspect was a man and Rachel, while tall, couldn't be mistaken for their suspect. "Selene's attacker isn't a woman."

"I get that, but Rachel hangs out with a rough crowd. If I were you, I'd check that out," Ralph said and emphasized it by pointing a long, thick index finger in his direction.

If there was one thing Robbie had learned over the many cases he'd worked with South Beach Security, it was to never ignore a lead. "I appreciate that, Ralph. We will check out Rachel."

With a definitive nod, Ralph said, "Is there anything else you need?"

Robbie met Selene's gaze, and she did a quick little shake of her head and stood. "I appreciate everything you've done, Ralph," she said and as Ralph lumbered to his feet, she hugged him hard.

The other man returned the embrace but glanced at Robbie over Selene's shoulder. "You take care of this lady."

"I will and we'll do what we can to fix things with the bar owner," Robbie said and shook Ralph's hand.

"Thank you. I'm going to deal with it as soon as I finish cleaning up," he said and tossed a hand in the direction of the dirty wall and broken glass.

With the interview finished, Robbie, Selene and Lily hiked down the four flights to street level where they took a few minutes to walk Lily to let her relieve herself. The snow had stopped and as they walked her, Selene said, "Do you think Rachel could be upset enough to want to hurt me?"

Even though it would both pain and worry her, he had to be truthful. "From what I've seen, people hurt each other even for no reason sometimes. It's worth checking out."

Selene said nothing, but there was no denying she was troubled by that possibility.

Because of that, he steered their conversation to another topic. "Time to head back to the condo. I have some work to do."

"And I have to do a last listen before I send the file to the producer."

The uncertainty in her voice rang loudly. He laid a hand on her shoulder and gave a reassuring squeeze. "I heard that recording at the studio and it sounded fabulous."

She offered him a forced smile. "It's just that… It means so much to me."

"I know, mi amor," he said, and as she turned to walk to the passenger seat, he enveloped her in his arms and hugged her tight. "Have faith. She's going to love it."

She murmured a "Mmm" and relaxed into his embrace for a second before she said, "We should go."

"And once we're both done with our work, we can decide on dinner, especially since we skipped lunch." As if to prove his point, his stomach did a loud grumble, jerking a laugh from Selene.

"You are definitely a bottomless pit," she teased yet again with a shake of her head and a lopsided smile.

"Yes, I am," he admitted. He hopped up into the driver's seat and started the SUV.

Ralph's place wasn't all that far away from the condo and gallery and barely ten minutes later they were home.

Selene pointed in the direction of her bedroom. "I'm going to listen in there. I don't want to disturb you."

He'd already told her that nothing could bother him when he worked. He suspected that she wanted some privacy to listen to the final files before she sent them. If she sent them.

He worried that with everything that was going on, her emotions might be quite fragile—enough that she would hesitate because of the fear of rejection.

But he had to have faith that she would do it because it meant so much to her. And in truth, to him, because if the producer did sign her, she'd likely go to Miami. That would give them time to explore and grow the relationship that had begun under such difficult circumstances.

As happy as he would be about that, he'd be sad that Sophie would not be making the return trip with him because of what was happening between her and CBI Agent Ryder Hunt. But as much as he might miss Sophie, what he wanted most was for her to be happy.

Armed with that, he yanked out his laptop and sent out an e-mail to his sister and the SBS team to ask them to dig up what they could on Rachel Ebbets. As he finished his e-mail, the faint strands of music drifted beyond the closed doors of Selene's bedroom.

Lily, ever the protective pittie, had assumed a position by the door, an almost happy grin on her face.

Was the dog enjoying the music too? He paused for a moment to listen and appreciate it. But that enjoyment was shattered as his phone pinged.

A text message from Sophie.

"Urgent. Need to talk to you about Jason Andrews. Are you free?"

Chapter Nineteen

Selene sat propped against the headboard, laptop next to her, eyes closed as she listened to the ballad—one of the three songs Jason and she had decided to send to the Miami music producer.

She loved the emotion in the song and the harmonies they'd worked up for the melody.

But in the back of her mind, Rachel's snub about the other ballad she'd wanted to record stuck in her craw. Were her songs too pedestrian and run-of-the-mill as Rachel had implied with her "speed" comment?

Worry destroyed her appreciation of the melody but as it finished and the faster, catchier tune started, that malaise faded, replaced by the satisfaction at what they'd accomplished.

Jason had done a great job of arranging the song she'd written and adding the instrumentals and harmonies they'd recorded just the day before.

She owed him a great deal and would have to find a way to repay him. What he charged her for his work and the recording studio was in no way enough for all that he had done.

As the song finished, lightness filled her, erasing the worrisome doubt that had plagued her just moments earlier.

She uploaded the files to a folder on the cloud, created a link for sharing and then opened her e-mail program. She searched her drive for the e-mails she had exchanged with the producer and drafted a short note to her, including the link so she could download the files.

Her finger hesitated over her touch pad and the send command.

With a deep inhale, she tapped the touch pad and sent the message.

Blowing out her breath in relief, she shut her laptop and was about to join Robbie when a sharp series of urgent taps sounded at her door.

She rushed over and jerked the door open.

The serious look on Robbie's face, lips tight and blue eyes dark with worry, warned she might not like what he was about to tell her.

"What's up?"

"You should come and sit down," he said. He clasped her hand and walked her to the sofa.

Lily followed them and with a sigh, settled herself at Selene's feet.

Selene sat and he took a spot beside her, her hand still held in his to offer comfort.

"What do you know about Jason?" he asked, and her hand trembled in his.

"I know he's on your list, but I've told you that you're barking up the wrong tree," she said and drew her hand from his.

She had argued against Jason being one of their unsubs and that made this discussion even harder.

"SBS tried running Jason through all their databases but couldn't find him anywhere."

Selene narrowed her gaze, her dark brows furrowed at his report. "What do you mean they couldn't find him?"

Robbie grasped her hand again and gently said, "There is no Jason Andrews. That's not his real name."

Selene's eyebrows shot up in surprise and were sharp slashes against her skin, which had paled with his announcement. "I don't understand."

"SBS could find no birth or other records for Jason Andrews. They reached out to Ryder, just in case they were maybe missing something, but his office confirmed they didn't have any records for him either."

Selene pulled back, in shock, and wagged her head back and forth in denial. Raising her hands in emphasis, she argued, "That's not possible. I mean, he has the studio. I send him money for the work he does, which must go to a bank account. So, he has to exist."

"SBS didn't find any bank accounts, Selene. How do you send the money?" Robbie pressed, his tone gentle because he understood how difficult this had to be for her.

"Paypal. I use his e-mail address," she said, her gaze confused and almost wounded.

"Okay. If you can let us have that, we'll run it and see what we can find," he said and clasped both her hands in his. "If it's a misunderstanding, we'll figure it out."

Her eyebrows shot up again as she asked, "And if it's not?"

"We will find out who he really is and if he's the one who wants to hurt you."

SELENE PICKED AT her pad thai, listlessly poking around the shrimp and noodles on her plate. She'd thought that taking Robbie to one of her favorite local restaurants would help boost her appetite and distract her from her worries about Jason.

Robbie hadn't pressed after she'd provided Jason's Paypal information but she suspected that he'd wanted to. He'd likely held back because he'd seen how upset she was about the revelation that the Jason Andrews she knew was a false identity.

In truth, she wanted to know why he was using a fake name as well.

"Why do you think Jason is using an alias?" she asked as she finally forked up a shrimp and some noodles and ate them.

Robbie paused with a forkful of drunken noodles halfway to his mouth. "Normally it's not for anything good, but don't people use stage names in the music industry?"

"Singers and DJs do but I don't think Jason does either of those," she admitted and was a little surprised that Robbie was giving Jason an excuse for his fake name.

She took another bite as Robbie thoughtfully chewed and considered what she'd said.

After he swallowed, he said, "When did you first meet Jason?"

She looked upward and firmed her lips as she tried to remember the exact date. With a shrug, she said, "Maybe a year ago. I came back to Denver after…" She paused, not sure what to call that part of her life. *Post-abduction? Finally free of her ex?* she wondered.

Robbie understood her hesitation and gave her an out. "So you're back home and starting a new career."

She nodded. "I had some old friends in town who were involved in the music scene. You met two of them—Sam and Monty."

Robbie smiled at the mention of the twins in her band. "They seem like nice guys."

Selene nodded enthusiastically. "Rhea and I have known them since high school. Part of it was the twin thing but we were all artsy and hung out together."

"They got you started in the music scene here?" he asked and sipped the Thai iced tea he'd ordered. The bright orange drink was a perfect choice for him since it was sweet and creamy, much like the way he liked his coffee.

"It did. They played with a couple of groups, and I sang backup with them while I worked on my own songs," she said and ate some more of her pad thai as her appetite slowly returned. The memories of the happiness she'd felt at finally following her dreams alleviated some of her worry about Jason's lies.

"Did you sing backup for Rachel?" he asked, dark brows raised in question.

She nodded. "I did it a couple of times when her band's regular backup singer was unavailable."

ROBBIE RECALLED WHAT Selene had told him earlier about the other woman. "I know Rachel had it rough. Partner takes off and leaves her with a baby. She's getting older and you arrive, fresh-faced and talented. You eventually replace her."

"But that has nothing to do with Jason. It was Sam and Monty who introduced me to him," Selene said.

From what he recalled of the two and their long history with Selene and her sister Rhea, he doubted they had known of Jason's deception when they'd recommended him.

"Why did they hook you up with Jason?" Robbie asked and forked up more of his drunken noodles. The combination of wide noodles, chili paste, basil, peppers and onions was tasty, especially combined with the duck he'd decided to add.

Selene swallowed her mouthful of pad thai. "I had worked up about half-a-dozen songs and rearranged some covers—"

She stopped at his questioning look and explained. "A cover is when you do an interpretation of someone else's song."

"Got it," Robbie said, and she continued.

"I had enough content to put together an album I could stream and burn onto CDs to sell at the bar. Jason had produced a few of the songs for a band Sam and Monty were working with and thought he did a great job."

"He did an excellent job with you also," Robbie had to admit.

Selene beat him to the punch. "Why would he do that and

also be trying to hurt me? Why would he burn down his own studio?"

Robbie knew it sounded strange and yet he'd seen his share of strange while working for SBS. "We had a case about two years ago where a developer was going to blow up his building to hide construction defects."

Selene mouthed a "Wow" and set her fork down. "That's... unbelievable."

"It is, but we were able to stop it," Robbie said, obvious pride in his voice.

"You love what you do," Selene said and narrowed her gaze to read his reply.

"I do. I never thought that's what I'd end up doing with my life but I'm happy about where I am. Who I'm with," he said, then reached across the table and took hold of her hand to drive the point home.

Selene smiled and her vivid blue eyes dazzled with undisguised joy. "I never thought this was where I'd be but I'm happy with it. With being here with you."

The waiter popped over at that moment and said, "May I take your plates and get you a dessert menu? Our coconut custard or banana roti are popular."

While Robbie's sweet tooth was intrigued by the possibility of dessert, what he wanted more than anything was to spend some time alone with Selene.

"Would you like dessert?" Robbie asked but as his gaze locked with hers, he realized that she had no interest in any sweets. Only him.

"I'm good," she said. In a rush, they paid the bill and hurried out of the restaurant.

The Thai restaurant was in the Larimer Square area and not all that far from the condo. They strolled, hand in hand, down a street where lights and colorful banners celebrating an upcoming beer festival added a celebratory air. The area was busy on a weekend night, packed with people eating at the various restaurants and popping in and out of the many small businesses.

As they passed a comedy club, the raucous sounds of laughter spilled out into the street.

"Someone's having a good time," Selene said with a happy smile.

"For sure," he said, just as tires screeched and a car jerked to an abrupt stop on the street beside them.

Robbie yanked on Selene's arm and pulled her behind him, protecting her body with his, but as a biker started shouting curses at the car's driver and shook his fist at the man, he realized it was just a routine traffic incident.

The biker picked up his bike, hopped back on and drove away.

The driver of the offending car slowly rolled into the intersection, followed by another car, but as the second car reached the intersection, the passenger's-side window drifted downward.

A rifle muzzle came into view and before Robbie could react, the *pop-pop* and impact against his body drove him and Selene backward.

The car took off with the squeal of tires as his knees weakened and he staggered.

He looked down at his chest, struggling to understand the bright splashes of color on his shirt that couldn't mask the pain.

Bystanders immediately circled them and Selene guided him into a nearby chair for the restaurant beside them.

"Robbie?" she asked, hands unsteady as they ran over his shoulders and arms. Eyes wide in surprise as she examined the front of his shirt.

"I'm okay," he said shakily and sucked in a breath to quell the adrenaline surging through his body.

"You should call the cops," a bystander said while someone else shoved a phone in his face and said, "I got video of it."

Robbie nodded and looked up at the young woman with the phone. "Would you mind sharing that with me?" he asked and at her nod, he tapped his phone to hers for the transfer.

"Thanks," he said and sluggishly got to his feet.

Someone must have called the police since a second later, the sound of sirens approaching filled the air. A patrol car pulled up in front of them and the two officers hurried out of the cruiser and to their side.

The surprise on their faces mirrored that on Selene's and probably his own.

He had no doubt that Selene's stalker was responsible, but why just paintballs? Why not bullets?

A police officer questioning him asked, "Any idea who would do this?"

He shook his head, not wanting the local police involved in their investigation. "No. Probably some kids doing one of those TikTok challenges."

The officers shared a dubious look but since there was nothing else they could do, they handed Robbie their business cards, returned to their cruiser and pulled away.

Selene plopped into a chair next to him and cradled his jaw. She ran her thumb across the dimple in his chin and said, "You could have been killed."

"But I wasn't," he said and bolted to his feet. "We should go home."

SELENE DIDN'T ARGUE with him. She'd heard that paintballs could really hurt from Sam and Monty, who used to go to paintball parks in high school.

Which made her say, "Sam and Monty used to do paint-ball."

Robbie forced a smile, clearly in pain as they hurried away

from Larimer Square and back to 16th Street. As they walked, people looked at him oddly, seeing the colorful splotches of paint on his shirt.

His strides were long and fast, forcing her to keep up with his quick pace until he realized she was barely keeping up and slowed down.

"Sorry, my mind was elsewhere," he said as his gaze drifted down to his shirt.

"How bad does it hurt?" she asked with a wince.

"Stings. A lot. It'll probably bruise but at least I'm alive," he said mindlessly.

Guilt filled her and, in a pained whisper, she said, "I'm sorry you're always getting hurt."

He stopped and seeing her pain, he went to wrap her in his arms but stopped to not stain her with the paint, which she assumed was still damp. "It's not your fault."

He could say that repeatedly but she would never believe it. But she wouldn't argue with him, knowing it would do no good.

She skimmed her hand down his arm and then they were in movement again, rushing to reach the condo.

They had barely entered when Robbie's phone rang and Lily barked at their arrival, jumping up to welcome her home.

She rubbed the pittie's head with both hands and quieted her as Robbie struggled to listen to whoever was on the phone.

"Hold up and let me put you on speaker."

With a sharp jab on the phone, Sophie's voice screamed across the line. "How is it that I find out from a TikTok post that my brother was shot?"

"It was just paintballs," he responded, downplaying the incident for his sister.

"But it could have been bullets," she retorted.

"Why wasn't it?" he said, shifting the discussion and forcing Sophie to go into investigator mode.

"He wants to terrorize," she said, more quietly and thoughtfully.

Ryder's voice drifted across the line. "He's playing with us. He likes the challenge."

"He does," Robbie said and looked over at her. "Selene's the target but the escalation isn't just about her now, right?"

"I think so. The MO has definitely changed," Ryder said.

"Selene mentioned that two of her friends and bandmates used to go to a paintball park. I think we should run them just in case. But I don't think they're involved," Robbie said.

Selene nodded and added, "Sam and Monty are longtime friends. I don't think they could do this."

"Regardless, we'll run them while we're still trying to get more info on Jason," Sophie said and then quickly tacked on, "We found out Jason was using a fake LLC to rent the space for his recording studio."

"Another dead end, I assume," Robbie said.

"Yes," Sophie said. Selene's heart sank with the news.

It seemed that for all the progress that they'd made, they were no closer to finding out who was responsible and more importantly, how to keep the people she loved safe.

"I'll send you what we have so you can put your eyes on it," Sophie said, and a few seconds later, she ended the call.

Robbie sat back in his chair, his shoulders in a decided droop.

"You okay?" she asked, sensing that he was as dejected as she was.

"I am. I'm going to go shower. I think the paint leaked through my shirt," he said and bolted out of the chair and from the room.

Chapter Twenty

Robbie needed time alone to take in everything that had happened.

He ripped off his paint-stained shirt, wadded it into a ball and tossed it into the bedroom trash can.

Peeling off the rest of his clothes, he dashed into the bathroom and turned on the water in the shower, getting it as hot as he could stand it before slipping in beneath the stream of water.

He winced as the water rained on the spots where the paintballs had hit him.

The areas were already purpling.

At least both sides of his body matched now, he thought ironically, but then the realization of what had happened smashed into him.

He could be dead right now.

They could have been bullets, would have been if the stalker hadn't wanted to play mental games with them.

His body shook and the hot water sluicing down his body did little to quell the chill that had erupted in his gut.

He wrapped his arms around himself and stood beneath the water, willing away the chill and the debilitating fear that had caused it.

Fear was the last thing you wanted during an investigation. Some thought fear made you careful. To him, fear brought hesitation and hesitation could mean death in the wrong situation.

Because of that, he drove himself to finish the shower and dry off, determined to resume his investigation of Jason and now, Selene's twin bandmates, Sam and Monty.

But as he entered the bedroom, nothing but the bath towel wrapped around his waist, he found Selene standing there, two mugs in her hand.

"I thought you might like something warm," she said and held the mug out to him with a hand that trembled as her gaze skipped across his body.

He took both mugs from her and set them on the night-stand. Grasping both of her hands in his, he drew her near. "I do want something warm," he said and then leaned in to brush gentle kisses across her face and then to the sensitive spot just beneath her ear.

"I want you," he said, needing to celebrate life and love and not let fear rule his life.

She moaned and the sound vibrated through him as she stepped against him and shifted her hands to lightly drift them across his chest. "I'm sorry you were hurt. Again."

"Sssh," he urged with a finger across her lips. He traced the edges of them and then replaced his finger with his lips, kissing her. Tasting the sweetness of her lips and life and love over and over.

She slipped her hands lower to the edges of the towel.

Cool air swept across his body before the heat of her hands replaced it.

He groaned and his body shook as she caressed him. Breaking from the kiss, he laid his forehead and looked down, watching as her long, elegant musician's fingers played him. She stroked him, building passion until they were both trembling and breathing heavily.

"I want to be in you," he husked against her lips.

"I want that too," she whispered, her voice raspy with passion.

Because one more caress might undo him, he grasped her hands and led her toward the bed.

As he retrieved a condom from his wallet, she pulled down the comforter and bed sheets and climbed into the center of the bed.

She lay there, waiting for him. Her gaze was dark with desire as she trailed it all across his body.

When she licked her lips, leaving them shiny and moist, his body shook and he nearly lost it.

Hurrying onto the bed, he lay on his back and slipped an arm around her waist to urge her to straddle his thighs, wanting her to have control over whatever happened between them. He handed her the condom and she tore the foil package open and then slowly eased it over his length, making his body shake as he fought for control.

CONTROL HAD BEEN elusive in Selene's earlier life. That Robbie understood that and had gifted her control during their lovemaking had tears shimmering in her gaze as she rose over him and slowly sank onto him.

He filled her, physically and emotionally.

She stilled, savoring that moment. That union.

With her gaze locked with his, she slid her hands along his torso, pausing to gently skim them across the purpling bruises from the paintball hits.

The first tear slipped down her cheek, but he softly said, "No, mi amor. Por favor, don't think about that. Think about our love."

Her body shook from the force of her emotions.

He was right. This moment had to be about life and love. *Not death*, she thought as she moved, loving him with her body. Riding him until both of them were shaking, and she was so on the edge that she stilled, prolonging the moment—not sure she could continue, exhausted physically and emotionally.

Rolling, he tenderly moved her to the mattress and cradled her cheek in one hand as he moved, driving into her. Offering sweet words of love in Spanish as he took them up, ever higher, until with one powerful surge, the release washed over them.

His breath was as rough as hers when he lay down next to her and urged her to her side, still joined with her.

"I wish we could stay like this forever," she said and raked her fingers through the wavy strands of his dark hair.

"We might starve," he teased, dragging a chuckle from her.

"That bottomless pit of yours," Selene said and bopped his nose playfully.

"Yes, and we skipped dessert," he said and groaned as he finally slipped out of her.

"I believe there's ice cream in the freezer," she said just as a soft whine came from outside the door. "Or we could pick up something when we walk Lily."

"That sounds like a plan," he said, and in a rush they cleaned up, dressed and opened the door.

Lily was immediately there, jumping up to greet them and then running to the door to signal that she needed a walk.

They grabbed jackets, leashed the pittie and hurried down to the street.

ROBBIE WAS HYPERVIGILANT as they exited onto 16th Street.

Someone had to have followed them to the Thai restaurant and lay in wait to do the paintball attack.

Robbie wasn't going to be so careless again. Instead of heading toward the streets near the capitol building, he directed them toward the pedestrian mall, which would keep them clear of any car drive-bys. Their stalker would either have to ride the bus that ran the length of 16th or use a bike. The bus wouldn't allow for an easy attack or escape so he kept his focus on the few bicyclists and pedestrians in the area.

All was calm as they took a short walk, giving Lily time

to relieve herself before going into a local pastry shop. They picked up some cannoli and hurried back to the condo.

Once inside, Selene said, "I'll make some espresso. I suspect you plan on working late and it might help."

"It will. I want to check out that video of the shooting and get more info on Sam, Monty and Jason," he said and headed to the dining table while Selene hurried to the kitchen to make the coffee and dish out the cannoli.

He pulled his laptop from his knapsack and set it up at the table, making himself comfortable so he could get to work. He logged in to his e-mail and checked to see if he had any additional reports from either Sophie or the SBS team.

His sister had forwarded the results of the investigations into Jason that had revealed his name was an alias. He noted that the team was continuing their work to try to identify him, much like he planned to do.

The burbling of the coffee in the espresso pot and the earthy aroma wafted over to him, warning that Selene would soon be over with the coffee and cannoli.

He shut down his laptop to focus on that and also ask Selene a few more questions before he jumped back online.

She hurried over seconds later with a tray of the cannoli, a demitasse cup and a larger mug with the espresso. Gesturing to the mug, which was adorned with a moose standing in a forest in a bright red union suit, she said, "I thought you might need more space for your milk and sugar."

He would, especially since he normally used condensed milk to make Cuban-style cortaditos. "Thanks. That'll help," he said and was also grateful as he picked up the small jug with the milk and realized she had heated it as well to keep his coffee from immediately getting ice cold.

She placed a plate with the cannoli in front of him and sat across from him, the dainty demitasse cup before her. With just her thumb and forefinger she raised the cup and took a bracing sip. "Whew, that'll keep me up for a while."

"Maybe you should lay off that sauce, babe," he teased in a growly voice and picked up his mug.

SELENE HAD ANOTHER small sip of her espresso and decided that he was maybe right. While she wanted to keep him company, the caffeine might be a little too much. Which had her wondering about what had happened earlier with Ralph.

"Speaking of sauce, do you think Ralph told the truth when he said he didn't drink the whiskey?" she asked, worry alive in her voice.

"I do," he said with conviction.

"I thought so too," she said, grateful that they were at least on the same page concerning that one thing.

"I don't think Sam and Monty have anything to do with what's happening," she said, and he didn't hesitate to agree.

"I'm with you on that but stranger things have happened."

"Like Jason Andrews not being a real person?" she asked and picked up her cannoli.

He did the same and took a bite. The crispy shell cracked as he bit it, and powdered sugar drifted to the tabletop. He wiped it clean with his napkin and around a mouthful of shell and cannoli cream said, "He's a real person, just not who he says he is. Did he ever mention anything about his past?"

"He did actually. I was talking about how Rhea and I used to ski near Regina—" she began and then stopped abruptly.

"I know I asked you all not to tell Rhea about what's happening on account of the baby, but what about that video Sophie saw? Do you think she'll be able to see it as well?" she said, panicked that it might cause her sister to worry and possibly cause harm to the baby.

"We asked everyone to keep this quiet but just to be on the safe side, I'll text Jax and give him a heads-up," he said.

He grabbed his phone and quickly shot off a message to his cousin.

Hoping that would be enough, she finished her earlier thought. "Jason mentioned that he never skied because he couldn't afford it, and it was too warm where he grew up. He said he spent his winters kneading dough to make dough," she said and rubbed her two fingers together in a money gesture.

"I'll check it out," Robbie said and popped the last bit of cannoli into his mouth.

She had yet to start hers and decided to rectify that mistake since the pastry shop was known for its amazing cannoli.

She bit into it and savored the sweet cream and chocolate chips as well as the crispy, flaky shell with the barest hint of sweetness from the marsala wine used to make the dough.

With a pleasurable sigh, she looked over and found Robbie watching her intently.

"You're cute with that powdered sugar all over your face," he said and eyed the last bit of her cannoli.

"You're just sweet-talking me to get the rest, aren't you?"

She leaned across the narrow width of the table and held the last bit of pastry up to his lips.

He steadied her hand and ate it, then playfully licked her thumb and forefinger clean of any cream or powdered sugar.

"Thank you," he said, voice hoarse, and jerked his head in the direction of the laptop. "I'm going to dig around and see what I can come up with on Jason."

Robbie grabbed his laptop and opened it, using it as a barrier to keep him from seeing Selene because she was just way too tempting.

Although their banter had been playful, he would have liked nothing more than to keep licking his way up to her lips and make love with her again.

But he had to keep her safe and that meant finding out who Jason Andrews really was.

The one clue that Selene had would not be easy. There had to be hundreds of bakeries in the several Southern states. The first thing he had to do was eliminate some areas. He hadn't detected a heavy drawl in Jason or heard any other giveaways, like "y'all." Because of that, he leaned toward Jason having grown up in a state like Florida, especially in the southern sections of the state that had seen an influx of Northeasterners and Latinos.

At first glance, he wouldn't say Jason was a Latino but since Latinos were a rainbow of races, it was possible. After all, the Gonzalez family with its Celtic Spanish roots was white with light eyes. His family's long presence in Cuba had also imparted other traits to them that lingered long after they escaped to Miami. That ethnic background could fit Jason, but his speech didn't have the singsong rhythms that tinged his Gonzalez cousins' speaking—the product of being bilingual. Of course, not every Latino Miamian had that accent.

Sophie and he had no accent because they'd grown up in the D.C. area, although their mother had that Cuban Miami rhythm in her speech.

Which had him leaning toward Jason being Caucasian, which wasn't much help. But he could at least ask his SBS team to generate a list of DMV entries of white men fitting Jason's general description from Florida's far south counties.

Something that Selene had said filtered back into his memory. He looked toward her where she lay on the nearby sofa, reading on her phone, Lily sprawled close to her.

"Selene," he said to draw her attention.

She lifted her gaze from her phone and he said, "Did Jason say that he kneaded dough to make dough in the winter?"

Nodding, she said, "Yes, he did. It made me wonder what he meant by that, and he said he worked at a bakery."

He tipped his head from side to side, considering that. Most bakeries made bread year-round and not just in the winter months. If Jason needed money, why not work all year and not just the winter? Unless it was a specialty bakery with a seasonal business.

A vague memory teased him of yeasty, sticky, sweet cinnamon buns that Julia, the SBS receptionist, had brought as her contribution during their annual holiday party.

Peering at his desktop, he realized it was past eleven at night. Not a good time to call Julia. He normally wouldn't hesitate to flag Trey but since Roni and he were dealing with a new baby and he didn't want to possibly wake it, he texted his cousin first.

Do you have time for a quick question? he wrote and waited.

While he did that, he ran an internet search and got an immediate hit for a bakery about an hour away from Miami. A bakery that was only open during the winter months and was quite popular.

A lead that might help them get Jason's real name.

His phone rang not a second later. Trey calling him. He immediately answered.

"Thanks for getting back to me, primo," he said to his cousin.

"Of course. I wish we had more info to give you at this end, but the team is still working on your unsub's real identity," Trey said in apology.

"Actually, I may have more for you based on something Selene remembered," he said and provided Trey with a report on what he had uncovered.

"I know which bakery you mean. It's only open during the winter and I'm sure that's where Julia got her buns. She lives in Kendall, which isn't far from there," Trey advised.

"Do you think you could make some calls and see if anyone remembers someone named Jason or someone who looks like him?" Robbie asked.

"We can work on that and, if we get a hit, check DMV to confirm we have our man," Trey said without hesitation.

"Gracias, primo. That would really help," Robbie said and after a brief exchange about how Roni and the baby were doing, Robbie ended the call.

"That sounded promising. Was it?" Selene asked.

Chapter Twenty-One

Selene didn't want to be too hopeful that Robbie had made progress since it seemed as if every time they tried to take a step forward, something bad happened.

Robbie nodded and shut down his laptop. "Possibly. I think I have a lead on where Jason—or whatever his name really is—worked in South Florida. Trey is going to call around and see where that leads."

"That's great," she said and as he rose and walked toward her, hand outstretched, she stood and tucked her hand into his.

Careful not to trip over Lily at her feet, she walked with him to her bedroom, the pittie chasing after them.

At the door, she released Robbie's hand long enough to give the dog a good body and head rub before commanding her to stay.

The ever-obedient pittie did as she asked and positioned herself at the door.

They walked in and Selene closed the door behind them for privacy. Silly really, but it was almost like having a child that she didn't want to see what Robbie and she were about to do. Which had her looking at Robbie and imagining what a child of theirs might look like.

Dark wavy hair, like both of them.

Light eyes definitely.

A dimpled chin like Robbie's, she hoped, with her smaller nose.

The musings brought a smile to her face and as Robbie did a side-eyed glance in her direction, he caught sight of that smile.

"I like seeing you happy. What were you thinking?" he asked and sat on the edge of the bed.

They were now eye to eye and there was no avoiding an answer. "I was thinking of babies…" she began. She hesitated and then lied to avoid it getting too serious. "Rhea and Jax. Your cousin Trey and his wife, Roni. So many new additions to your family."

He circled her waist in his hands and drew her into the cradle created by his thighs. "Have you ever thought about babies of your own?"

She didn't want to keep on lying. "I did. With you," she finally admitted.

His hands shook and his blue gaze darkened to the gray of storms sweeping across the nearby mountains.

He licked his lips and with a slow nod, he said, "Maybe once this is all over, mi amor."

Leaning in, he kissed her, sealing that promise and she gave herself over to him and the love and hope he had brought into her life.

Hope she hadn't expected. She almost didn't want to believe it was possible after all she'd suffered.

But she wasn't going to doubt it anymore.

She embraced it, and him, with every fiber of her being.

As they undressed, her hands lingered over his body, soothing his injuries the way he'd soothed the pain in her soul.

When they came together, she wrapped her arms and legs around him, never wanting to let him go.

ROBBIE STILLED, SAVORING THE feel of her body surrounding him. Savoring the comfort and completeness of her embrace.

He'd never thought of himself as being alone or lacking

anything in his life. After all, he'd been surrounded by his loving family and was financially secure.

But Selene filled a previously unknown hole in his life and as he drove them toward their release, he knew he had to have her in his life forever.

"Te quiero, mi amor," he said, professing his love for her.

She skimmed a hand across his cheek and gave him that beautiful, joyous smile again. "I love you too."

Moved beyond words, he shifted inside her, pushing for that final, satisfying union. Calling out her name with a rough breath as he lost control and buried himself deep in her warmth.

Her body arched as she shattered against him, accepting his body and his love.

He braced his arms on either side of her, keeping his full weight off her body, but she slipped her hands up to his back and urged him down.

"I want you close," she said and whispered a kiss across the side of his face.

Slowly he eased down and then urged them to their sides, content to rest beside her. Allowing himself to let go of all that was happening to just treasure the moment.

Long minutes passed and her soft, even breath spilled against where she had buried her head against his chest.

Lulled by that, he let himself drift off to sleep.

THEY HAD JUST finished taking Lily for a post-breakfast walk when Robbie answered a call from Ryder and Sophie.

"Let me put you on speaker," he said and placed his phone in the middle of the table.

Selene unleashed Lily, rubbed her head and urged her to sit as she took a spot at the table.

At her nod, Robbie said, "We're good to go."

"We got the results of the handwriting analysis just a few

minutes ago. The expert believes that there are significant similarities between Jason's handwriting and that on the threatening letters," Ryder advised.

Selene's stomach did a weird drop and clench with the news. She laid a hand there to quell the desire to vomit. "Are you sure?" she asked shakily past the bile rising in her throat.

"The expert is sure. Granted, it's finesse things we're talking about, like how certain letters are finished. Some hooks and lines here and there," Sophie advised.

Selene peered in Robbie's direction. Deep furrows marred his forehead as he processed the news. "What does this mean? Is it enough to get a search warrant?"

"I'm uncomfortable with relying on just this. I'm told we should have the DNA results on that rope from beneath the stage by this afternoon. If that's a match, I'll head straight to the district attorney for not only a search warrant. I'll ask for an arrest warrant," Ryder advised.

Robbie bobbed his head and said, "We have news as well. With some info that Selene remembered, we think we have a lead on Jason's real identity. Trey is working on it this morning and we hope to hear from him soon."

"That's great, Robbie. It sounds like a lot is coming together," Sophie said and in the background, the sounds of activity filtered in.

"Sorry, but I have to go. I've got another case with a hot lead, but Sophie is going to wait here for those DNA results," Ryder said and Sophie tacked on, "I'll call as soon as we have anything."

"Great. We'll keep you posted as well," Robbie said and ended the call.

As soon as he did so, he reached across the table and gently undid the fist she hadn't even realized she'd made.

Her gaze locked with his as she said, "Why? Why would

he do this? He's been nothing but supportive and you heard the amazing work he did for me."

With a huge lift of his shoulders, he said, "Dr. Jekyll and Mr. Hyde? It's been my experience that you never really know what's in someone's head."

Dr. Jekyll and Mr. Hyde definitely fit Jason if the rest of their investigations confirmed that he was the one behind the letters and attacks. But despite the evidence that was slowly coming out, it was still hard for her to imagine that Jason wanted to hurt her.

Shaking her head, which sent strands of her hair shifting back and forth across her shoulders, she said, "I can't believe it, Robbie. I just can't."

He squeezed her hand, offering comfort. "Let's wait until we know more. In the meantime, what else can you tell me about Jason?"

She shrugged and said, "He works hard. The studio isn't his only gig."

"WHAT ELSE DOES he do?" Robbie asked, his voice calm and soothing to not ramp up Selene's upset. Despite his perception of Jason, Selene had always had faith in him.

Selene hesitated and worried her lower lip. After thinking about it for a few seconds, she said, "He helps out with some of the local arts groups. I also think he does some kind of work with a local amusement park, and he lives there."

"He lives at an amusement park?" Robbie asked, eyes wide in surprise.

With a bob of her head, she said, "Kind of. It's a small town nearby where it's mostly people who work at the park. I think there's also a big-box store and strip mall there."

"Have you been there to visit him?" Robbie asked, wondering just how friendly Selene and Jason might have been.

She immediately shook her head. "No. Never. There was

no reason to visit him but Rhea and I have been to the amusement park often. It's like a landmark."

"Can you give me the address?" he asked while reaching for his laptop.

"Sure. I had to mail something to him once and jotted down the address," she said and whipped her phone from her back pocket. She swiped her elegant musician's fingers across the screen and then read off the address.

Robbie entered it into one of the mapping services and then pulled up a satellite view. Turning his laptop so he could see it, he motioned with his finger to the areas on the screen.

"It looks like he lives right next to the park and this speedway, which looks pretty rough," he said, examining the satellite images of what appeared to be a large parking lot with a series of crumbling buildings and a grandstand.

Selene nodded and said, "It's been closed for as long as I can remember. Why does it worry you?"

Robbie ran his finger all along the buildings and then to the large parking lot that opened into the amusement park. "It's a big area to cover with lots of possible hiding places."

Selene skipped her gaze all across the screen and circled her finger in the area of the speedway. "It looks like a lot of area, but it's fenced off."

Robbie swung the laptop back around and perused the screen again. As good as the satellite and street mapping programs were, there was one even better thing.

He shut his laptop with a loud slam and said, "I think it's time for a road trip."

Chapter Twenty-Two

It was a short fifteen-minute ride from the condo to the Lake-side area.

Robbie slowed the car as they neared Jason's home and Selene spotted Jason's old army-green Jeep sitting in front of a shack-like home located next to the speedway and amusement park.

A fence topped with barbed wire surrounded the speedway, which took up a good amount of land on one side of the road. The opposite side of the street had several small stores and strip malls.

As Robbie turned onto another road, they went past a gas station and ended up in the parking lot for a large strip mall with a fitness center, restaurants, storage units and a big-box retailer.

Turning back toward the speedway, he returned to the street for Jason's home. There were several other small homes along the boulevard in various states of care. Interspersed with them were fast-food restaurants, chain pharmacies and, about a hundred yards away, the entrance to the amusement park.

Since it had yet to open for the season, the gates were closed and the marquee welcomed patrons to come back in the spring. Several yards ahead, some of the park's colorful kiddie rides were visible from the street but closed off by fencing.

The sight of them brought memories of Rhea and her visiting with their parents. She gestured to one ride. "Rhea and I used to go on those teacups until we realized Rhea had really bad motion sickness," she said with a laugh.

"Sophie has the same problem and she's not a fan of heights either, so we didn't do many rides. But we loved hitting the arcades, which I guess explains why we developed some gaming apps," Robbie said with a wistful smile and turned onto a side street by the end of the park.

A large white roller coaster ran from the street corner and down the road to a large lake along the perimeter of the park and some scattered, small business buildings. At the end of the street, Robbie turned back toward the strip mall they'd found earlier.

"I don't know about you, but I'm hungry and we still have to wait on Ryder," he said and glanced in her direction.

"Bottomless," she teased with a smile.

Unfazed, Robbie turned into the strip mall parking lot and drove down to the restaurant but it didn't have outdoor seating and they weren't going to leave Lily behind, who had been patiently harnessed in the back seat.

"Backup plan. There was a fast-food place back on the main road with outside tables," Robbie said. He did a K-turn and backtracked to that restaurant.

But as he turned into the parking lot, his phone rang.

Trey was calling.

ROBBIE TAPPED THE screen and Trey's voice crackled across the line.

"That lead was gold, Robbie. We visited the bakery and they identified him," Trey said, excitement ringing in his voice.

"That's great news," Robbie said and sent a side-eyed glance at Selene, who breathed a sigh of relief.

But that relief was short-lived as Trey said, "He's got a record. Stalking. Terroristic threats. I'm sending it all to Ryder and I hope that gives him enough for at least a search warrant. I'll copy you on the e-mail."

"Thanks, Trey. Selene and I will review it as soon as we get it," he said and ended the call.

He unbuckled and turned slightly in the seat to see her.

The earlier happiness of remembering good times in the amusement park was gone, replaced by fear. Her face had paled and was downcast. She clasped her hands tightly, her knuckles white from the pressure.

He covered her hands with one of his. "I know it doesn't seem like good news, but it is."

She slowly raised her head to meet his gaze. "It doesn't feel that way, Robbie."

A ping on his phone warned that Trey's e-mail had arrived. He pulled the phone from its holder and flipped it open to enlarge the screen. With a few swipes, he opened the e-mail and its attachments, but because of Selene's fragile state, he decided to review the materials first.

He was glad he did.

Jason's real name was Jason Anderson Forrest. He'd owned a recording studio in the Miami area before a divorce settlement had drained his finances and forced him to liquidate his assets. The rift that had ended the marriage had gotten worse after the divorce, with Jason regularly harassing and threatening his ex-wife.

A protective order had seemingly ended that, but Jason had then turned his attention to several other women according to police records. The pattern of alarming notes and physical intimidation had gotten progressively worse until an arrest warrant had been issued in one of the cases.

The Florida warrant was outstanding—probably because Jason had fled as far as he could and adopted a new identity with money he'd stolen from one of his last victims.

Drawing in a deep breath, he blew it out in a disgusted

gust as he finally turned his phone so Selene could read the documents.

She was silent as she took it all in, her finger trembling as she swiped the screen to move from one document to another. When she was done, she wrapped her arms around herself and said, "Why?"

Why? He wondered what she meant until it hit him.

Why did she always end up with men who would hurt her? Except he would never do that.

Snapping the flip phone closed, he skimmed the back of his hand across her cheek, comforting her. "He's not going to get to you again."

She nodded, but stared straight ahead, lost in her thoughts.

In the back seat, Lily whined, sensing Selene's upset, and Robbie reached back and rubbed the pittie's head to reassure her. "It's okay, Lily. It is," he said and the dog quieted.

Returning his attention to Selene, he stroked his hand across her shoulders and said, "Ryder should have enough for a search warrant now."

With a sharp heave of her shoulders, she said, "Will that be enough to stop him?"

She was in denial, and he got it. Her life had been upended again and until Jason was behind bars, either here or in Florida, she wouldn't have peace or control once more.

"Once they're inside his home, they may find that stationery. The paintball gun. Other things that will tie him to the attacks," he explained patiently.

"You're mansplaining and that's not what I meant," she shot back angrily. Whirling to face him, her gaze bore holes into him with her focus and anger.

"What I meant was… I'm tired of living my life in fear. I want to control my life. I want Jason out of it. Now," she said, leaving no doubt about what she was feeling.

He held back from reassuring her because she didn't need

it. Her determination was clear from the way she'd straightened her shoulders and lifted her head a notch.

His phone rang again. Ryder this time.

He swiped to answer and said, "Tell me you have good news."

"We do. The DNA came back and confirmed it was Jason. With the info that Trey sent, I have enough to go to the district attorney for an arrest warrant," Ryder said.

Robbie raked his fingers through his hair, worried about any kind of delay. "How long will that take? Because if Jason decides to rabbit—"

"I can't make any promises, but hopefully not more than an hour or so," Ryder advised.

Their gazes locked and as if their minds were in sync, she nodded as he said, "We're not far from Jason's home. We're heading there and will keep an eye out for him."

Ryder's response was immediate. "Do not do anything stupid."

Sophie jumped onto the line to echo the statement. "Por favor, Robbie. Stay put. We're on the way and Ryder has already contacted the local police department to send backup."

"Got it," Robbie said and ended the call, but not because he agreed.

"Buckle up," he said. He started the car and quickly headed back in the direction of the amusement park and the small line of homes beside it.

When he neared, he drove by more slowly and confirmed that the shack-like structure with the older Jeep in front of it was Jason's home. At the light, he executed a U-turn during a break in traffic and approached the shack but stayed several yards away from it and Jason's Jeep. He didn't want to draw any unwanted attention and alert Jason that they were onto him.

But he wasn't going to be caught flat-footed either.

Unbuckling, he reached behind to free Lily from her harness and commanded her into the front seat, where the pittie immediately plopped into Selene's lap.

"Good girl?" Selene said doubtfully with a puzzled look.

"I want her free to protect you," he explained and stroked the back of his hand across her cheek.

Not a breath later, Selene said, "He's leaving."

Robbie whirled just as Jason bounded out of his house and down the walk, a happy-go-lucky smile on his face. A bouncy jump in his step. But as he neared the street, he suddenly peered in their direction.

He stopped dead as his smile disappeared and his face seemed to transform before Robbie's eyes. Dr. Jekyll was gone and Mr. Hyde had taken his place.

Jason whirled and dashed toward the home's backyard.

Chapter Twenty-Three

"Stay here. Call Ryder. Fill him in," he said. He handed her his phone and bolted from the car to chase after Jason.

He raced to the house just in time to see Jason scrambling up the fence closing off the park from the public. Someone had cut away the barbed wire, making it easy for Jason to climb up and flip over the fence onto the closed park grounds. Jason ran down the paved road between the park and the speedway, heading straight to the roller coaster by the lake.

Robbie grabbed the wire of the fence and sped to the top and over, landing with a hard awkward jolt that reverberated through the assorted aches and pains in his body. Ignoring that, he chased after Jason but lost sight of him as Jason disappeared into the ruins of the abandoned raceway buildings.

SELENE HAD DONE as Robbie had asked. She had called Ryder and alerted him to the fact that Jason had gone on the run.

She'd stayed put even as a police cruiser had pulled up behind her and she'd directed the officers in the direction where she'd seen Jason and Robbie disappear behind the house.

And then she'd sat there, impatiently waiting. Frustrated and worried all at the same time.

Much as she'd told Robbie, she hated not having control over her life.

Just like what was happening now as she sat and waited for others to set her free of the threat Jason presented.

She muttered a curse, grabbed Lily's leash and exited the car, determined to be the mistress of her fate.

Walking along the street, she kept an eye on the police officers as they searched in and around the kiddie rides and a building by the roller coaster.

There was no sign of either Robbie or Jason, which chilled her gut with fear.

While it seemed that Jason relished terrorizing more than actual hurt, he had almost killed them in the stage collapse. If cornered, would he kill Robbie?

She didn't want to be one of those too-stupid-to-live heroines she'd seen often in a novel or movie, but she wasn't going to let anything happen to Robbie either. Not when she'd finally found love.

Just beyond the row of small homes, the fence line for the abandoned speedway met up with the sidewalk. She knew she couldn't go up and over the barbed wire.

Lily yanked at her leash, pulling her forward, and about a hundred feet farther up, there was a gate secured with a thick, heavy metal chain and padlock. But the gate hung sufficiently askew, allowing Lily to sneak through the gap. Selene followed the pittie, squeezing through the gaping doors, the rough metal edges snagging the fleece of her jacket.

But she got through and with no sign of either Jason or Robbie, she hesitated, unsure of where to go. As Lily pulled at her leash, she said, "Sit, Lily. Sit."

The dog immediately complied, and Selene searched the area, wondering where Jason and Robbie had gone. The police officers were still in the amusement park, searching that area.

There were no signs of anyone in the abandoned speedway, but then an idea hit her.

"Where's Robbie, Lily? Where is he?" she asked the dog.

Lily's ears perked up and Selene repeated her request. "Find, Robbie, Lily. Find Robbie."

The dog jumped to her feet and jerked on the leash, pulling Selene in the direction of the abandoned buildings of the grandstand.

Selene raced after her, trusting the pittie's sense of smell. Hoping the dog had understood her command and would lead her to Robbie.

ROBBIE GINGERLY INCHED up onto the sagging floorboards of what had once been one of the grandstands for the speedway. The wood was silvery in age in some spots that had been long exposed to the elements, while the more protected areas still bore traces of the white and red paint that had once graced the grandstand.

The weak wood groaned beneath his weight, giving away where he might be, so he backed off it onto the ground.

Weeds and grasses had grown up in and around the grandstands and along the edges of the oval dirt track where cars had once raced.

There were scuffs in the dirt track. *Footsteps, like someone racing away*, Robbie thought and glanced in the direction of where they led to a grandstand area to his right.

Jason was nowhere to be found.

Robbie thought about following outright, but hesitated, certain that Jason would be waiting for him to do just that and attack as soon as he was near.

Instead, he doubled back to where he'd entered the central grandstand and moved along the edges there, careful not to step on any of the pieces of wood or other debris that might alert Jason to his whereabouts.

As he neared the end of the one grandstand, he heard a snap. He stopped. Held his breath. Listened.

A loud rustle. Yards in front of him.

A second later there was the barest flash of brightness by the back of the grandstand.

White like the T-shirt Jason had been wearing beneath his denim jacket when he'd sauntered out of his home.

He hurried in that direction, careful not to give away his position.

But Jason must have heard him since he dashed from the grandstand area and rushed out into the weed-strewn parking lot.

Jason was about to run away from the amusement park and to the far side of the speedway, but loud barking froze him in place.

Lily, Robbie thought and rushed out into the open.

Selene and Lily stood about a hundred feet away, closing off Jason's escape across the speedway lot.

Realizing that, Jason took off in the opposite direction, straight for the amusement park.

LILY BARKED AND pulled at her leash as she saw Robbie and Jason, almost jerking Selene's arm from its socket.

Seeing her and Selene as he emerged from the deteriorating grandstands, Jason took off in the opposite direction to make his escape.

Robbie gave chase, and with another powerful yank, Lily pulled her leash from Selene's hand and raced after them too.

Selene ran after the pittie, falling farther and farther behind, unable to keep up with Lily's speed and the distance between herself, Robbie and Jason.

Yards ahead of her and Robbie, Jason veered toward the street but suddenly the two officers were there again, emerging from the kiddie section.

Realizing that his avenue of escape to the street was foreclosed, Jason stopped short and then dashed in the direction of the roller coaster and lake.

In her mind's eye, she recalled what they'd seen as they'd driven and how the coaster ran for a good distance along not only the lake but the side street.

If Jason could outrun both Robbie and the police, he might be able to make his escape in that direction.

As Jason slipped beneath the infrastructure for the roller coaster and then climbed up on the track, Robbie followed.

Her heart leaped into her chest as the two men climbed ever higher on the tracks.

Lily had stopped by the coaster and was looking upward and barking loudly, drawing the police officer's attention to what was happening.

The two officers raced in the direction of the ride.

LILY'S BARKING DRIFTED up to him as he chased after Jason, careful not to slip on the tracks of the wooden coaster or fall between the gaps of the structure.

He looked down only once—in time to see Selene reach Lily and grab hold of her leash. She was joined by the two police officers and the faint squawk of their radios said they were calling for backup.

Distracted, he missed a step and had to grab a side rail to keep from falling between the cracks and to the ground. The rough edges of the wood bit into his hand but it could have been worse.

Focus, he told himself, especially as a sudden feeling of vertigo crashed over him.

He better understood Sophie's fear of heights now.

Jason clambered ever higher, knowing his only way of escape was to reach the length of the roller coaster and then drop down to street level.

Sucking in a shaky breath and stabilizing himself on the track, Robbie sped upward.

His breath was rough as he climbed ever higher, his gaze

shifting from the coaster tracks to Jason, whose dark denim jacket and white shirt blended with the white and dark of the roller coaster. It made it hard to follow him, especially as the infrastructure became a maze of side rails, support beams and tracks.

Focus, he warned again as his sneakered feet slipped on slick wood.

Ahead of him, Jason was nearly at the peak before the drop.

Robbie had to reach him, had to stop him before he made his descent that might lead to escape. Especially since the two police officers were stretched thin, one standing by Selene while the other one was scrambling around on the coaster tracks ahead of them.

Robbie pushed, racing ever closer, and he was barely a few yards away when Jason reached the peak and suddenly disappeared on the downward dip.

He cursed and continued his pursuit. As he neared the peak, Jason was nowhere to be found.

Muttering another expletive, worried that he'd lost the other man, he took a step to move downward and suddenly his feet were sliding out from beneath him.

He'd misjudged just how steep the dip was, and he had to grab the side rails to not go tumbling down the slope or through the gaps in the tracks.

Righting himself, he realized Jason had not been as lucky.

The other man barely had a hold of the track and dangled in the air precariously, nearly eighty feet in the air.

Robbie eased over and stared between the tracks at Jason's face, white with fear.

"Don't let me fall, please don't let me fall," he pleaded.

Robbie had only seconds to act before Jason lost his grip.

Fearing that Jason might pull him down, Robbie laid his

body down along the tracks and opened his legs to brace them on the lower side rails.

Reaching between the tracks, he grabbed hold of the front of Jason's jacket and pulled.

Chapter Twenty-Four

Selene held her breath as Jason and Robbie reached the highest peaks of the roller coaster.

She gasped as Jason fell through the cracks between the tracks and dangled in the air.

The fall would kill him.

A second later, Robbie slipped from view and fear gripped her as she searched for him in the tangle of rails and tracks of the ride.

But then he popped up and reached Jason.

Please, Robbie, please, she thought, praying he could stay safe but save her attacker.

When she lost sight of Robbie, she moved closer, trying to get a better view of where he was.

The police officer at her side radioed for EMTs, as if certain that the situation wasn't going to end well for one or both men.

As she slipped beneath the infrastructure, she caught sight of Jason and Robbie as well as the second police officer, who was heading up the tracks from the opposite end of the coaster.

Robbie had grabbed hold of Jason's jacket and was trying to pull him back up onto the ride.

Jason was struggling to hold on and his one hand slipped off the wood, but then grabbed hold of Robbie's arm.

But how long could Jason keep that grip? Worse, could Robbie avoid being pulled down if Jason fell?

Please, Lord, please, she prayed silently and then mere seconds later, a second set of hands grabbed Jason's jacket.

The police officer had finally reached Robbie and Jason.

Together Robbie and the police officer pulled Jason to safety.

Barely minutes later, the three men were visible at the peak, and she finally breathed a sigh of relief.

Slowly, the three made their way down the tracks just as the sounds of sirens split the late afternoon air.

An ambulance, police cruiser and unmarked car pulled up to the curb.

Officers and EMTs spilled from the cruiser and ambulance while Ryder and Sophie emerged from the unmarked car.

Spotting her, the couple raced to her side.

"He's okay," Selene said as Sophie searched the coaster for any sign of her brother.

As Robbie slipped onto the ground, Lily broke free and raced in his direction. The pittie jumped up on Robbie as he emerged from beneath the infrastructure, a handcuffed Jason and police officer following him.

Selene and Sophie rushed over, and Selene threw herself into Robbie's arms, dragging a pained *oomph* from him from the force of her embrace.

ROBBIE HELD SELENE, rocked her and stared past her shoulder to where his sister stood, tears in her eyes, but also ice-cold anger.

"What part of 'Don't do anything stupid' did you not understand?" she asked, but then she was joining their embrace, hugging him and Selene.

"It all worked out," Ryder said as he approached and laid a hand on Sophie's shoulder.

Sophie and Selene stepped back as Ryder said, "Jason Anderson Forrest, you're under arrest for attempted murder, stalking and menacing." He then read Jason his Miranda rights and turned him over to the police officers to take Jason to a local police station.

Once the officers were on their way, Ryder faced them. "I'm going to head over to the station and make sure we button this up."

"What if he lawyers up?" Sophie asked, obviously worried about that possibility.

"We'll deal with it if he does. I'll meet you back at Rhea's condo as soon as we're done," Ryder said and hugged her before walking off to follow the police officers and Jason.

Sophie faced him and said, "Are you sure you're okay?"

His arms were a little sore from pulling Jason up and he might have a splinter or two, but otherwise there was nothing, so he nodded and said, "I'm okay. Let's head back to the condo and let Trey know we can close this case."

He circled his arm around Selene's waist and with a gentle nudge, urged her in the direction of their car.

BACK AT THE CONDO, Selene poured them all coffee as they prepped to call SBS in Miami and give them an update.

Robbie was about to start the video call when Selene's phone rang.

She narrowed her gaze at the sight of the unfamiliar number but as Robbie peered at her phone, he said, "Three-oh-five is a Miami area code."

Miami. Maybe even the producer, which she hoped was a good sign.

Hands shaking so badly she almost couldn't swipe, she finally answered.

"Hello," she said, voice trembling.

"Selene Reilly. This is Teresa Alvarez. How are you?" the woman said. She had a take charge tone in a raspy voice, as if from too many cigarettes or a cold.

"I'm well, thanks. Were you able to download the files okay?" she asked, not sure of what else to say.

"I was and I have to say, I love your style and the songs," Teresa said and that was followed by a pause that weakened Selene's knees, driving her to sit down because she knew what was coming next.

"But I don't think you'll fit into my stable of artists. However, I have a dear friend, and I sent him the link. Do you know Rip Bradley?"

Everyone in the music industry knows him, Selene thought and murmured a "Yes. Of course."

"He'd like to chat and if you have a moment, I can conference him in," Teresa advised, but she didn't wait for Selene's approval.

The line seemed to go dead for a hot second and then both Teresa and Rip were on the line. Her mind whirled as the duo talked about her signing with Rip as if they had to convince her to work with one of the biggest producers in the business.

"I'd like that. Sure," she said, agreeing to look over the contract that Rip was going to send over as soon as they finished the call.

Robbie sat beside her and met her gaze as she ended the conversation and lowered the phone.

He gently grasped her shoulder and squeezed. "Is everything okay?"

Sophie took a spot beside her brother, face filled with concern, and Selene finally said, "The Miami producer isn't interested, but she's connected me with someone who is."

"Is that a good thing?" Robbie asked, eyes narrowed as he examined her as if trying to figure out what she was feeling.

It was a good thing except for the fact that she would no longer be going to Miami.

"The producer is here in Denver," she said, meeting his

gaze which grew dark with the realization that they might soon be separated.

"Oh," was all he said.

The dual ping of their phones echoed in the silence of her announcement.

The siblings glanced at them and almost in unison said, "It's Trey. He's waiting for us to start the meeting."

It was a welcome interruption since she didn't have a clue as to how to deal with the joy and pain twining together in her heart at the thought of reaching for her dreams at the expense of her relationship with Robbie.

The siblings were subdued as Trey, Mia and Ricky popped onto the video feed, broad smiles on their faces, which faded as they took in their cousins' demeanor.

"Everything okay? I thought you'd be happy that we identified Selene's stalker," Trey said to start the meeting.

"We are. He's in custody and we're waiting on Ryder to let us know how the interrogation went," Sophie advised and snuck a peek at Robbie.

"It's just that Selene has had some good news," Robbie said, not that there was anything about his tone that screamed happy.

"Y'all don't look as if it's good news," Mia said, her gaze drifting over their faces.

"The Miami producer passed on me but connected me with a well-known Denver producer who wants to sign me," Selene explained, and it was as if a light bulb went off in his cousins' heads.

"I guess you won't be coming to Miami," Trey said and then quickly added, "Sophie's floated the idea of staying in Denver, but what about you, Robbie?"

Robbie hesitated and then peered at Selene as he said, "I was thinking about it if Selene wants me to stay."

Selene smiled and clasped his hand tightly. "Of course I

want you to stay. I love you," she said, loudly and without hesitation.

A loud sigh of relief escaped him, and he nodded. "I'd like to stay in Denver if that's good with all of you."

The three cousins shared a look and then Trey said, "We've been expanding SBS in a variety of ways. Why not a Denver branch? You two can work remotely on Miami cases but also bring us investigations in the Mountain states."

"Are you sure?" Sophie asked, wanting to make sure their cousins were truly on board with them remaining in Colorado.

"One hundred percent sure. We would never do anything to keep you two from being happy," Trey said and his siblings echoed their agreement.

Mia held up a finger to stop further discussion and said, "We just need one thing from you: a name for the new branch."

Robbie and Sophie laughed and glanced at each other. Something seemed to pass between them, much the same way that Rhea and she often shared something without saying a word.

"How about Crooked Pass?" Sophie said and Robbie quickly added, "It's the name of our favorite ski slope in Regina."

Trey smiled and said, "Crooked Pass Security. It has a good ring to it."

"And I suspect there will be lots of other rings happening soon," Ricky said with a happy smile as his gaze drifted from Sophie to Robbie and then landed on Selene.

Robbie grinned and as his gaze met Selene's, he said, "You might be right."

"It sounds like there's not much else you need right now, so we'll let you go," Trey said and ended the call.

After he did, Selene clasped Robbie's hand. "Are you sure this is what you want to do? I know how important family and your work is to you."

With a side-eyed glance at Sophie, who smiled at him, Robbie said, "It'll be exciting for Sophie and me to set up the new branch." He waited for a heartbeat and then blurted out, "And you're family too, but I want it to be more. I love you. I want to spend the rest of my life with you if that's what you want."

If you had asked her even months ago if she was ready for another relationship, the answer would have been a resounding no.

But nothing could have prepared her for the man sitting next to her. A kind, caring and strong man who had shown that he could handle just about everything.

"It's what I want, Robbie. More than anything," she said and leaned forward to seal their love with a kiss.

"That's my clue to go. Hopefully, Ryder will be home soon too," Sophie said. She hopped to her feet and rushed to the door.

Robbie and Selene joined her there, hand in hand. Robbie hugged his sister hard and said, "I can't wait to start this new adventure with you."

Sophie smiled and returned the embrace. "Ditto. It's going to be great to get Crooked Pass Security off the ground."

Once she was gone, Robbie faced Selene and clasped both her hands. "I know it probably wasn't the kind of proposal you imagined—"

She laid a finger on his lips to stop him. "I'd never imagined being in another relationship. But you've shown me that love is possible for me again and that's more important than any fancy proposal."

His grin erupted beneath her finger and his sea-blue eyes glittered with joy. "Still, I'd like to make it fancy and special so if you don't mind, I'd like us to go find a ring and then go to dinner. Alberto's since that's the first place we went to dinner together."

She chuckled and shook her head. "Liar. You just want Bart to see the ring on my finger."

He laughed as well and shook his head. "Am I that transparent?"

She nodded. "Yes, and you know what else I see?"

"What?" he immediately retorted.

"That you will always make me smile and keep me safe. But more importantly, that you will always love and respect me," she said, then grasped his hand and tugged it playfully.

"I can't argue with that. I will always love and respect you," he said and kissed her as if to seal that promise.

"I know," she said, sure that their life together would always be filled with love and respect—*and lots of food*, she thought as his stomach grumbled loudly, warning that it was time for a meal.

"Bottomless," she teased. She signaled Lily to come to her side and together they all walked out of the condo and into their new life together.

* * * * *